"Ryder Do[...]
Really Am,

Savannah said between sobs to Hannah, the Malone family housekeeper, as Ryder's announcement rang in her ears. *I'm proud to introduce my fiancée....*

"I've loved Ryder since high school, but I looked different back then, and he doesn't recognize me. And just two nights ago we'd...we'd— Oh, Hannah...I thought he cared about me—" Embarrassed, Savannah stopped and the sobs came faster.

The housekeeper had sucked in air with each new revelation, her eyes wide and her hand covering her mouth. "Savannah, you've got to tell the man the truth—everything. That...*woman* can't make my Ryder happy. You mark my words—a mistake has been made. And a mistake can be fixed. You just hush those sobs, miss."

Savannah forced a small smile, a tiny ray of hope in her heart.

Dear Reader,

A book from Joan Hohl is always a delight, so I'm thrilled that this month we have her latest MAN OF THE MONTH, *A Memorable Man*. Naturally, this story is chock-full of Joan's trademark sensuality *and* it's got some wonderful plot twists that are sure to please you!

Also this month, Cindy Gerard's latest in her NORTHERN LIGHTS BRIDES series, *A Bride for Crimson Falls*, and Beverly Barton's "Southern sizzle" is highlighted in *A Child of Her Own*. Anne Eames has the wonderful ability to combine sensuality and humor, and *A Marriage Made in Joeville* features this talent.

The Baby Blizzard by Caroline Cross is sure to melt your heart this month—it's an extraordinary love story with a hero and heroine you'll never forget! And the month is completed with a sexy romp by Diana Mars, *Matchmaking Mona*.

In months to come, look for spectacular Silhouette Desire books by Diana Palmer, Jennifer Greene, Lass Small and many other fantastic Desire stars! And I'm always here to listen to your thoughts and opinions about the books. You can write to me at the address below.

Enjoy! I wish you hours of happy reading!

Lucia Macro

Lucia Macro
Senior Editor

Please address questions and book requests to:
Silhouette Reader Service
U.S.: 3010 Walden Ave., P.O. Box 1325, Buffalo, NY 14269
Canadian: P.O. Box 609, Fort Erie, Ont. L2A 5X3

ANNE EAMES
A MARRIAGE
MADE IN JOEVILLE

SILHOUETTE *Desire*®
Published by Silhouette Books
America's Publisher of Contemporary Romance

To the most beautiful Savannah of all.

 SILHOUETTE BOOKS

ISBN 0-373-76078-7

A MARRIAGE MADE IN JOEVILLE

Copyright © 1997 by Creative Business Services, Inc.

Books by Anne Eames

Silhouette Desire

Two Weddings and a Bride #996
You're What?! #1025
Christmas Elopement #1042
* *A Marriage Made in Joeville* #1078

*The Montana Malones

ANNE EAMES

joined Romance Writers of America in 1991 and set a
five-year goal: to sell her first novel. A year ahead of
schedule, Anne sold *Two Weddings and a Bride*, followed quickly by *You're What?!* and *Christmas
Elopement*. As a bonus, her debut novel landed on the
USA Today bestseller list the same day that Silhouette
bought her fourth novel, *A Marriage Made in Joeville*.

Anne and her engineer husband, Bill, live in southeast-
ern Michigan, and share a blended family of five—two
hers (Tim and Tom), two his (Erin and David) and one
theirs (an adorable miniature dachshund, Punkin).

Dear Reader,

When I first embarked on this trilogy set in Montana, I nearly panicked. The closest I'd ever been to this state was watching *Legends of the Fall* (and even then I noticed more of Brad Pitt than the scenery)! So the research began, and soon I had videos and maps and beautiful photo books strewn all over my office. Before I realized what was happening, I'd fallen in love with an area I had barely thought about previously. And the next thing I knew, my husband, Bill, and I were on a plane headed for Bozeman, Montana, with a string of bed-and-breakfast reservations covering points east and south. I hope in reading my next three stories, you will experience some of the beauty and grandeur we enjoyed during our travels through this truly awesome state.

In book one of The Montana Malones, you will meet Ryder and Savannah, once high school best friends, reunited after twelve years of separation. (You might want a box of tissues handy for this one.) Also in this book, you'll get to know the rest of the family: brothers Shane and Joshua, and their father, Maxwell Malone, a semiretired orthopedic surgeon with secrets of his own that are interwoven into all three books. And then there's Hannah, the cantankerous housekeeper, plus Bucking Horse, a member of the Crow tribe who lives on the ranch and manages to wield his influence over more than the horses that he trains.

I hope you enjoy The Montana Malones and that these people become as real to you as they have become to me.

I love to hear from readers! So for those who write and enclose a self-addressed stamped envelope, I will send along a little surprise. In the meantime, a special "thank you" to each and every one of you for taking my books to the *USA Today* bestseller list. It's loyal readers like yourself who have made another dream come true.

Warmest regards,

Anne Eames

Anne Eames
Write c/o: 4217 Highland Road #252
Waterford, MI 48328

Prologue

"**A** lotta good it did to save myself, huh?" Savannah folded a pair of jeans and slapped them into her suitcase. "All these years of waiting for the right guy and another one bites the dust." She flung a couple of sweatshirts in the general vicinity of the bed.

Jenny leaned against the doorjamb and crossed her arms. "At least the wedding invitations weren't sent out yet."

Savannah stopped packing and dropped cross-legged on the braided oval rug. "He could have told me a long time ago there was someone else." She shook her head, feeling the familiar sting of betrayal.

"You told me you weren't sure he was the one, anyway. So why the long face?"

Savannah bowed her head, the heat of a sudden blush traveling up her neck. She stole a peek at Jenny's cocked eyebrow, then lowered her gaze again. "Because now I'm the dumpee, not the dumper." And after a lifetime of self-doubts, she still felt like that frumpy little fat girl of her youth, regardless of her metamorphosis.

"I'd prefer to think you made the decision and he simply forced your hand." Jenny's tone softened as she pushed off the jamb and moved closer. "All things considered, isn't it for the best?"

Savannah glanced up and caught Jenny's tender look. "I guess so." Then with more enthusiasm, she added, "You're right, as usual."

Jenny nodded her head and knelt down. "Smart girl." After a brief reflection, she tugged at Savannah's arm and pulled them both to their feet.

"Come on, kiddo. That was over a month ago. No point beating yourself up over it again." She wrapped an arm around Savannah's shoulder and ushered her to the white wicker love seat angled in the corner of the room. They sat sideways on overstuffed chintz cushions, tucked their legs beneath them and eyed each other.

"Tell me, Jen. Have you ever been passionately in love? You know, the kind of goose-bumpy feeling whenever he walks into a room, or brushes a part of you accidentally?"

Jen looked away with exaggerated wistfulness, then back in a flash. "No."

"Never?"

"Passionately in lust? Oh, yeah. But not what you're talking about."

"Maybe I'm the incurable romantic for holding out so long, but geesh, Jen, somebody better come along pretty soon. I'm almost thirty, for Pete's sake!" She let out a self-deprecating chuckle. "I can almost hear my mother saying, 'If you don't use it, it'll get rusty.'"

"Your mother." Jenny rolled her eyes. "Now *there's* a woman to emulate. Where exactly in Europe is she this month?"

"This isn't about my mother." Savannah heard the defensiveness in her voice and was surprised it was there. Jenny had every reason to sound critical of a mother who'd abandoned a teenage daughter before the ink was dry on her father's life insurance check.

Jenny poked Savannah's knee with an index finger.

"Sorry. Shouldn't have dug up that old bone." She squirmed in the corner of the sofa in a way that left no doubt they were changing the subject. In an airy, optimistic voice she said, "Look at it this way, something good came out of it. At long last you're going to Montana to check out this passionate love I've been hearing about."

Savannah looked across the clothes-strewn bed and wondered if her latest decision had been the right one...or just another impulsive folly.

"You don't look too convinced, amigo," Jenny said, looking askance. "Okay, let's go through it one more time." She turned and faced Savannah squarely. "In the seven years since I've known you, who do we end up talking about every time you break up with another guy?"

Savannah grabbed the pillow next to her and hugged it to her chest.

"Come on. Say it."

"Ryder. Ryder Malone." Savannah peeked out from under her lashes, her heart skipping faster at the mere mention of Ryder's name. Amazing. Twelve years since he'd left Detroit, and he still had this powerful effect on her. "But you keep forgetting something, Jen. I was just his buddy, nothing more." She expelled a weary sigh. "Time's marched on. I'd be lucky if he even remembered me."

"You know he'd remember you. That's not why you're worried." She scooted closer and patted Savannah's knee. "You're afraid he won't care."

"You don't pull any punches, do you?"

"I'm your friend, remember?" She tilted her head lower and waited for eye contact.

Savannah rewarded her with a smile. "How could I forget?" She squeezed Jenny's hand then pushed off the love seat. "I'll never get my packing done at this rate. And we still have that haircut and dye job to do." She reached back and pulled Jenny's hand. "Come on, *friend.* Get your butt in gear. You talked me into this little charade. The least you can do is help."

Now it was Jenny's turn to look dejected. She stood motionless in front of a wicker armrest.

"What? What did I say?" Savannah stared at the moisture rimming above Jenny's lower lashes.

"I know it's the right thing…you going to Montana, taking that job, getting to know Ryder again…but, God, Savannah. This apartment is going to seem awfully empty without you."

"It's just for the summer, maybe less—"

"No," Jenny interrupted. "You're never coming back." She swept at a lone tear with the back of her hand.

The simple statement sucked Savannah's breath away. Not the words, but the certainty with which they'd been spoken. Jenny had a way of saying things as though they were fact. And with an eerie insight she never quite understood, Savannah knew Jenny was always right when she used that distant, unwavering tone. She'd joke it was the Crow thing—the one-half native American blood that channeled through her veins, sending prophetic messages to her brain. Whatever it was, it rocked Savannah to the core. She lowered herself onto the foot of the bed.

"You could always move to Joeville with me," Savannah said, not thinking for a second it would happen, but not wanting the separation, either. Jenny had been more than a friend. She'd been the sister Savannah never had, her confidante, her own personal clairvoyant. Even if things went perfectly with Ryder, which she found hard to believe, she couldn't imagine going months or years without seeing her best friend.

Jenny sniffed and walked toward the headboard. "Ha! Could you picture me in Joeville, Montana? With all those cowboys and Indians?"

Yes, she could, but more importantly she didn't miss the use of the word *Indians*. Jenny's political incorrectness was intentional. It always was whenever her ancestry entered the conversation. Her father's abandonment and mother's bitterness toward an entire race had hung over Jenny like a large gray cloud in the shape of giant question mark. No.

That wasn't true. Only Savannah saw the cloud as a question mark. Jenny wouldn't allow herself to question. To question was to bleed some more.

Jenny lifted a maroon and gold volume from the nightstand, finding the diversion she sought, and turned back with a devilish smile. "Hmm. What have we here? Class of '85—"

"Oh, please. Don't." Savannah winced and prepared for the inevitable.

Jenny thumbed to the index in the back. "Let's see...senior photo, page twenty-seven." She fanned the pages backward, then stopped and covered her mouth with her hand. "So *this* is why you never showed me!"

"I know, I know. What a sight, huh?" Savannah crossed to Jenny's side and grimaced at the image of her former self: braces, shoulder-length mousy brown hair, and at least an extra fifty pounds.

Jenny looked from the photo to Savannah then back to the page. "Too bad you don't wear contacts so we could change those baby blues to green." Looking up again, she said, "Still, just a little more work and he'll never know it's you." She put the book down and swept Savannah's hair back from her face with both hands. "Yep. Shorter and darker ought to do the trick."

"Let's do it now...before I lose my nerve." They looked into each other's eyes a moment, then burst into nervous laughter as they scurried for the bathroom, pushing and poking each other as they went, pretending to forget goodbyes were less than twenty-four hours away.

Savannah shed her sweater, settled atop the toilet seat and made a pocket with the towel Jenny pinned around her neck to catch the clippings.

"Should we do medium length first or go for broke?"

She looked up at Jenny's blue-black hair. It was cropped short with jagged ends trailing slightly down her neck. Equally jagged bangs and sides all pointed to large, doelike brown eyes. If she could look half as good as her friend with this same style, she'd be happy.

"Just like yours."

"You're sure about this?" Jenny tested the shears with a couple of quick snips in midair.

"Just hurry up. Do it." Savannah closed her eyes and held the towel out around her.

A half hour later, her butt numb from the hard plastic lid, and her arms aching from catching all the hair, she blew air at a stray lock that itched her nose. "When can I see?"

Jenny unpinned the towel and carefully removed it. "Hold your horses. I'm a long way from finished." She slipped on disposable plastic gloves and went to work with the pointy-nosed bottle of dye. "We can pack during the twenty-five minutes this goop is on your head."

She finished in a flurry, then removed the gloves and fanned her face. "Gadzooks! You look worse than that stuff smells." She chuckled and grabbed her friend's hand, tugging her back toward the bedroom. "Okay, let's pack...and no peeking." Savannah started to turn toward the mirror, but Jenny nudged her forward and shut the bathroom door behind them. "Now, about these clothes you're taking—"

"What's wrong with my clothes?"

"They look like you."

"I can't afford a whole new wardrobe—"

"No, but you could take a few of my things."

"They're a size too small!"

"Exactly. What's the last thing Ryder would expect the old Savannah to wear?"

She looked at her bulky sweaters and oversize flannel shirts flung on the bed. She liked clothes loose and comfortable. She never felt secure showing off her more-than-ample bust, which to her own eyes seemed disproportionate to the rest of her trimmer self. "You can't possibly mean for me—"

"To wear tight tank tops or form-fitting blouses? Yep. Trust me. It's just what you need."

When Jenny left the room, no doubt to retrieve her sexier clothes, Savannah looked down at the open yearbook and turned to Ryder's photo, her heart beating erratically once again.

Was disguising herself the right thing to do? True, she didn't want him to know who she was till the time was right…if that day ever came. First, she wanted to study the man he'd become, to see if he was anything like the fantasy she'd lived with for so long. And she wanted him to get to know her again, too, without his feeling some sense of obligation to be kind to an old friend. Anything less than honest feelings would be a waste of time.

Honest. What a dichotomy. She hated being dishonest with Ryder, yet she saw no other way of learning the truth.

She focused on his photo again and remembered the other thing that worried her. National Locators had found where he lived and told her about the job opening at the ranch. They'd also said he wasn't married. But what if he was involved with someone? After all of this, what would she do?

She closed the book with a resounding thud. She didn't want to think about it. She had enough on her mind, least of which was the ridiculous job she'd be applying for once she found the ranch.

Jenny rushed back into the room, a smile from ear to ear and clothes draped across both extended arms.

Savannah laughed and accepted the offering. "Okay, I'll take a few of your things. *Maybe* I'll even use them."

They continued emptying drawers and the closet, filling another suitcase with underwear, nightshirts and shoes, while Savannah continued fretting about the week ahead. "Jenny, do you really think I can pull off this cook job? I've never been anything but a secretary at Detroit Tire."

"The one and same warehouse that laid you off with a couple of hundred others. Don't you think that was another sign this was meant to be?"

That *had* seemed rather fortuitous. She never liked that job, anyway, and had recently sent out résumés. "Still, you're the one who cooks for a living. I'm the one who nukes and does carryout."

"You got about a dozen basic meals down pat, and there's lots more in that cookbook I gave you. If you get in a jam, I'm only a phone call away." She looked at her watch. "Time to hit the shower. Close your eyes."

Savannah stripped with her back to the mirror while the water warmed. When she stepped inside, she lowered her head under the spray and watched dark brown water swirl around the drain at her feet. Another ball of anxiety gripped her stomach. Of all the hare-brained ideas she'd had over the years, this one had to take the cake. She lathered quickly and rinsed. A new persona, a new part of the country she'd never seen, and a job she knew little about. With a groan, she shut off the water and stepped out.

Jenny stood waiting—blow dryer in one hand, brush in the other, and the ever-present look of caring in those big brown eyes. God, how she'd miss this woman. Tears blurred her vision, and she blotted them away as she dried herself and tied the bath sheet into a large knot at one side.

"All right," she said on a sigh. She shot Jenny a dubious glance, then did her best to sound lighthearted. "I'm ready. Work your magic."

With the heavy scent of coconut mousse filling the air and every available surface cluttered with makeup, Jenny ran to the next room and back, getting what she said was the perfect outfit to finish the picture. Playing along, Savannah shrugged into a too-small rust-colored tank top, tucked it into a tight fitting pair of cutoffs and spun toward the mirror for the long-awaited unveiling.

"Oh…my…God." She fell back a step, not recognizing the image in front of her. "I look like a totally shameless slut!"

Jenny looked at their reflections and shook her head back and forth. "Uh-uh." Finally, she turned her friend around, gripped her by the shoulders and spoke sternly. "Savannah Elizabeth Smith…you look drop-dead gorgeous."

Savannah puffed out her cheeks, exhaled a loud breath and stole another peek over her shoulder. "Isn't it a little on the trashy side?"

"Sure, but you're going to Montana, remember?" Jenny laughed at her own joke, then stepped back and admired her work. "Cowboys like their women a little on the trashy side. Hell, there's even a song that says so."

Savannah rolled her eyes and chuckled nervously. "Yeah, I think I heard it a while back."

"Then relax, girlfriend. Everything's going to work out just the way you want it." Jenny pulled her into a tight embrace and laughed over her shoulder. "Yep," she said, thumping Savannah's back and rocking her side to side. "Ryder Malone won't know what hit him."

One

Dawn broke over the familiar pair of snow-crested mountains to the east, bringing Ryder Malone to a rolling stop on his favorite promontory. He cut the ignition to his pickup, opened the door and stepped outside, the pungent, clean scent of sage filling his nostrils.

Spring in Montana. A time for hope, new beginnings. The cynic in him said he was crazy to think anything different would happen this year, that something or someone would fill the hole in his soul he'd almost learned to live with. He'd survived another winter. It was as simple as that.

Still, coming home to live under the same roof with the man he blamed for his dour disposition, had to make some kind of difference. Good or bad, it remained to be seen.

He walked to the edge of the rough sandstone bluff and looked out over the rolling plains of the ranch below. Home. Too infrequently, he felt the meaning of the word. Until last month there had been only brief visits during college and after that, eight years of working at a ranch hundreds of miles to the north. Not since before high school days in Detroit had he actually lived here. Yet something still drew him back, some part of him felt this was home.

He arched his back, the stiffness lingering from another sleepless night on Maddy's lumpy sofa bed. He stretched and yawned loudly, knowing the velvet-antlered deer a few yards away couldn't care less. They watched him cautiously, but didn't skitter off as he stared back, his thoughts drifting to Maddy and little Billy. He couldn't think of one without the other. He pictured the freckle-faced towhead with a missing front tooth and the area around his heart constricted. There was so much pain ahead for that little guy. How would he ever...

Ryder blinked and looked at the front gate, letting it pull his focus outward, away from a problem that couldn't be fixed today. A large arch spelled out the words: The Montana Malones. Beyond the scattered livestock, he viewed the main house—a sprawling log building, an addition at the back rising a story above the original structure, virtually tripling the living space. There were private quarters for the housekeeper, Hannah, plus his younger brother, Joshua, and himself. There was space for Shane, too, but he preferred living with Bucking Horse in the small cabin behind the stables, where the old Crow had taught the firstborn everything he knew about horses. Their father had his own wing in the main house, separate from his three sons. As usual. Shane had probably made the right decision, Ryder thought, an old anger welling up inside him. If there had been room in the little cabin, he would have stayed there, too. But there wasn't.

Smoke puffed from the chimney in the kitchen, and his stomach growled. The others would be at the table by now, Hannah hovering over them in her typical mother hen fashion. If he hurried, breakfast would be hot and plentiful. But hurrying held no appeal this morning. The warm spring sun, rising in the sky, casting shadows on his favorite twin mountains, did. He walked ahead, his gaze fixed.

He'd always thought the rugged cliffs looked like two giant molars, a pair of large *M*s mirrored cleanly in the still waters that lay peacefully in front of them—two *M*s that signaled the settling place for the Montana Malones. At least that's what his great-granddaddy had written in his journal all those years ago. In spite of all else, it was a sight he never grew weary of watching. It was an ever-changing view, yet a constant in times of turmoil. On days like today, there seemed little point in dredging up the past. His father had hurt them all as boys—not so much with his words, but with his absence.

And other things.

But he was no longer a boy, Ryder reminded himself, resuming his stroll, and the old man was nearing retirement. Maybe it was time to let it go. Besides, his father had nothing to do with his reasons for moving back to the ranch. Shane's letter had provided the last nudge he needed to move closer to little Billy. He'd written that Joshua planned to start a farm soon, leaving too much for Shane to manage. So big brother had reminded him in not-too-subtle terms that, since each stood to inherit a third of the ranch someday, it seemed only fitting he begin pulling his own weight. And Shane was right. Besides, he had no beef with his brothers, and the years and distance had made them practically strangers. The time was right on all fronts for things to change.

Ryder stopped and sat gingerly on the precipice, dangled his feet over the edge and spotted a small cloud of dust miles down the road. He watched the car move closer, idly wondering who it might be so early on a Monday morning. But then his thoughts returned to his brothers...and finally to young Billy. Never far from his thoughts was poor Billy.

"This is the last batch," Hannah groused, dropping another platter of pancakes in the center of the table. "It's not like cookin' is the only thing I gotta do 'round here, ya know." She grabbed a coffee urn off a side table and made the rounds refilling cups. "And another thing, if I don't get help pretty soon, yer gonna trip over me lyin' on the floor one day."

"Now, Hannah." Max wiped his mouth with a cloth napkin and tried to look stern at his housekeeper of nearly forty years. "I told you last night, we have another young woman coming out this morning." He looked at his watch: 5:45 a.m. "In fact, she should be here any time."

"Young woman?" Joshua arched a brow.

Max smiled at his youngest son, who eyed him with a hopeful grin over the rim of his coffee. "Well, she sounded young."

"Everyone sounds young to you." Shane snapped, sharing a knowing look with his brother, before stabbing a couple of pancakes off the platter.

"I don't see where it matters one way or t'other," Hannah said. "She'd just be another hired hand, not some plaything for you boys."

Max watched the exchange between his sons. At thirty-two and twenty-five, they were hardly what he'd call boys. But to Hannah, he knew, they always would be. He glanced over at the empty seat and frowned. They may be men now, but his middle son still acted like a middle child. Where was he this time? Or with whom, was more the point?

"Maybe that's her now." Hannah stood at the window with a stack of empty bowls in both hands. "I'll go see."

Max stood abruptly. "No. I'll take care of it this time."

Hannah didn't budge. "You? Whadaya know about cookin', anyhoo?"

"Not a damn thing...except how to hire someone who can." He softened his tone, not having meant to sound so brusque. Still, Hannah had scared away at least six women so far. He wasn't about to make this one number seven. He lowered his chin and raised his eyebrows. "Let me handle it, okay?"

"Humph." She spun on her heel and headed for the kitchen, not looking too convinced she shouldn't be involved.

Shane and Joshua craned their necks for a better view of the path to the door, but Max waved them back to their food, not wanting their interference, either. He ignored their complaints as he closed the double doors to the dining room and headed for the front of the house.

A once white Grand Am made its way up the dusty road and finally came to a stop at the end of the bark-strewn walk to the porch. Max sighed and rolled his eyes heavenward when the latest candidate stepped from the car. She was young, all right, and too damn good-looking. Not for himself, but for the three men he'd never been able to keep in tow. He watched her smooth her short, tight denim skirt down another inch, which still left it high above her knees. Her peach knit top fit snugly, leaving nothing to the imagination. Hannah would have his hide if he hired this one. Yet how much longer could Hannah handle everything on her own?

Max walked down the path to greet the young woman, seeing a warm and genuine smile lighting her face as he grew near. A good omen, he decided. Friendly counted for a lot in these parts. If she could string two words together in a halfway acceptable fashion, he'd offer her the job.

Savannah gave one last tug at Jenny's embarrassing skirt, then pasted on her best smile and walked toward the man she assumed was Max Malone—the one and same person she'd spoken to on the phone last night; the one and same person she'd heard so much about in high school. Two more steps and she thought she saw Ryder's dark eyes in his father's, an observation that made her stomach do another cartwheel. How was she ever going to pull this off? The man stopped a yard in front of her and extended a hand.

"Max Malone. You must be Essie."

She grasped his large, but smooth, hand and pumped it enthusiastically, grateful his gaze stayed at eye level. She'd kill Jenny for her silly stunt—substituting all of her smaller clothes for Savannah's more modest wardrobe. What must this man be thinking?

"Well, you passed the first two tests." His laugh was

warm and easy. "You found the place and made it here by six a.m."

She wouldn't tell him she'd left the motel at four-thirty, or how many wrong turns she'd made before she got it right. She was here and that's what counted. "Yes, and I brought the reference letter I mentioned on the phone. I hope one is enough." He looked over his shoulder at the house, then back.

"Do you mind if we talk outside for a while? I'm afraid I don't get out of my office as often as I'd like...and it's such a beautiful day."

"Your office?"

"I'm a doctor. I see a few patients in my office at the back of the house. The paperwork is what keeps me inside, not the number of patients." She nodded her understanding as he took her letter and gestured to the bench behind him. The wide seat was thick, weathered wood, held up on either side by large wagon wheels. She preceded him and sat carefully, keeping her knees locked together and pointed in the opposite direction from Ryder's father, who sat sideways beside her, crossing an ankle over a knee. He read the letter slowly, his gaze traveling back to the top of the page.

"S. E. Smith. Is that how you came to be called Essie?"

He was rereading Jenny's souped-up letter, which gave her a moment to regroup. She'd never told him her name was Essie. He must have heard it that way when she said S. E. on the phone. Essie. Essie Smith. Not her favorite, but it would work.

"Yes, that's right. Odd little name, but it's mine." She widened her smile.

"I bet the S stands for something you're not too crazy about." He looked up at last, his face tanned and handsome. And very much like Ryder's.

She pulled herself back to the conversation. "Y-yes." She waved her hand in a dismissive way. "You know, sometimes old family names are...well, out of step with the present." This was never going to work.

"Where do you live, Essie?"

"Uh...well, I'm new to the area." She'd practiced this one earlier, deciding to avoid any mention of Michigan on the off chance he'd play the old do-you-happen-to-know game. "Been staying at the Big Beak Motel till I find a job, then I'll get a place close by."

"Big Beak? That's quite a hike from here. Have you considered working as live-in help? I mean...if you find something you like."

She laughed before she answered. "Haven't seen too many apartment buildings around." She hadn't seen much of anything around. "Yes. If someone has room and makes an offer, I probably would."

Max slapped his knees and stood abruptly. "Well, Essie, your letter says you can cook, and we're in dire need of help. But in all fairness to you, maybe you should come in and meet the brood, look around before you decide. How would you like to join us for breakfast? There's bound to be something left."

Just like that. She had the job. It's what she wanted, but now that it was time to go inside and meet the "brood" as he'd put it, she found it difficult to swallow, let alone move. Would Ryder recognize her? Would the jig be up before it was started? She took a deep breath and exhaled slowly.

"Thank you. I'd love to. Just let me get my purse." She turned and walked back to her car. Through the rear window she saw a pickup truck barreling down on her and she jumped clear of the vehicle. There was no sign of the driver slowing. He was going to hit her car.

She stumbled backward onto the bark walkway, waving dust from her face and holding her breath. Brakes squealed and the back end of the pickup swerved. But it stopped inches from her bumper. Out jumped a rumpled-looking cowboy, his Stetson low over mirrored sunglasses. He strode toward her with a long, deliberate gait, a cocky swagger that reeked of arrogance.

"Well, well. What do we have here?"

"I hope we have a new cook...if you don't scare her off

before she steps foot in the place.'' Max scowled at the cowboy.

Essie crossed her arms across her chest—first, because she didn't like his attitude, and second, because the glasses were aimed at her cleavage. The cowboy removed his hat and beat it against his faded jeans, sending more dust in her direction. With one hand he raked his fingers through his tangled brown hair, and with the other, removed his shades.

She gaped at the familiar face, her heart sinking to her shaking knees.

"Sorry all to hell, ma'am," he said, his scowl now fixed on his father. "Any grub left?"

"Last time I looked there was plenty." Max looked around his son. "Essie, this is my son, Ryder. You'll have to excuse his manners." He looked back to Ryder. "Or lack of them."

Savannah watched the pair glowering at each other as though she didn't exist, their anger so transparent she felt embarrassed witnessing it. More than that, she felt sad. After all these years, she'd hoped this part of Ryder's life had changed.

Finally, Ryder glanced over his shoulder at her, his jaw muscles knotting. Then without a word, he looked away and started for the front door. Savannah stared after him, swallowing the lump at the back of her throat. This wasn't what she'd hoped to find. Not even close.

"Coming, Essie?" Max held out his arm and waited for her to pass.

As far as she was concerned, she should crawl into her car and head back to Michigan. She'd seen enough to know Ryder wasn't a man ready for *any* relationship. The chip she'd remembered in high school had only grown larger with time. But Max was standing there, smiling and waiting patiently for her to join them. She hadn't eaten much last night and hadn't had time this morning. Okay, she decided. One good breakfast and she was out of here.

Then she could forget about cooking.

Forget about Montana.

And once and for all forget about Ryder Malone.

She smiled at Max and preceded him into the house, with each heavy step trying to muster up some anger to replace the pain of her bitter disappointment.

Max seated Essie at the side of the long table, before taking his place next to her at the head, looking every inch the patriarch of the family. More uncomfortable than ever, her gaze flitted from the gaping men to the mounds of food on the table. Her chin dropped as she took in the spread— eggs, bacon, sausage, toast, pancakes, some mush that looked like oatmeal, muffins and fresh-squeezed orange juice. If she had any doubts before, looking at the amount of food on the table confirmed her decision to get out of Dodge while she could. This was a disaster waiting to happen. She'd never cooked this much food in a month, let alone at one time. She tugged at the back of her tank top, which hiked the front a little higher, fully aware that while she was staring at the food, the men were looking elsewhere.

"Essie, I'd like you to meet my other two sons." Max gestured to the far end of the table. "There on the end is Shane. He's the oldest. And next to him is Joshua, the youngest."

Joshua was first to perk up. "It's nice meeting you, Essie." He rose from his chair and moved to the side table. Holding up the urn, he asked, "Would you like some coffee?"

"Yes, thank you." Well, at least one of them had manners.

Joshua poured while Shane studied her silently. She took a sip of coffee and looked at the oldest brother again. He was still blatantly staring at her and didn't blink an eye when she caught him. It was as though he had thirty seconds to size her up and he wasn't going to miss his deadline.

Ryder had gone to wash up and change clothes, he'd

said, which added to her suspicion that he had probably just arrived home from the night before. It could have been with the guys, she told herself when he returned, his dark brown hair even darker around the wet edges, the ends skimming the collar of his fresh, blue chambray shirt. She eyed the empty chair across from her, hoping he'd sit there instead of in the one next to her.

No such luck.

When he sat next to her, she decided it was easier to avoid him this way, which she did. With words, anyway. Unfortunately, her pulse had a mind of its own. He had grown taller since school and seemed more solid, less lanky. She didn't have to look at him to feel his nearness. She was certain the slightest movement of her leg would make contact with his. Max passed her a platter of sausage, and she forked a couple of links, forcing her attention back to food.

"If that's not hot enough, I'll have Hannah warm it for you."

Hannah? There was already a cook in the kitchen? Working as a kitchen helper didn't sound nearly as intimidating. But what did it matter? She wasn't staying, anyway. She tested the sausage. "This is fine. Thanks."

Without invitation, Ryder tossed a piece of toast on her plate. She eyed his long fingers as they busied themselves at his own plate. Slow, sure movements. She managed to empty her mouth without choking and drank more coffee.

"Whatsa matter? Ya don't like my toast?" Essie jumped, not having noticed the older, portly woman who had entered the room behind her.

"N-no. I mean…I was just waiting for someone to pass me the jelly," she lied.

"Jelly!" Hannah shouted. "That's not *jelly!* It took me hours to put up strawberries. Them's *preserves,* young lady. *Not* jelly."

"Oh, for crying out loud, Hannah. You sound like that silly commercial." Max glowered at her, sending her a clear message to behave herself. "Hannah, this is Essie

Smith.'' Hannah walked closer and scowled at the appli-
cant, her formidable frame sending off waves of instant
disapproval.

Essie pushed out her chair and stood, tugging at her skirt
before extending her hand. "Nice to meet you, Hannah."
Her hand hung out there, untouched, as Hannah's fists
stayed put on her barrel hips. Essie just smiled and waited.
Things hadn't gone exactly as she'd planned so far, but she
would win this one if it took all day. Finally she saw Hannah's squinted eyelids flicker. Then, grudgingly, a chafed,
stubby hand grasped hers and gave it one hearty shake.
Essie exhaled the breath she'd been holding.

"Can I help you clear the table?"

Hannah shrugged. "If ya want." The woman waddled
back through the kitchen door, muttering under her breath.

"Don't mind Hannah," Max said. "Her bark's worse
than her bite."

Hope to God I never find out, Essie thought, shaking off
the mental image of a set of dentures embedded in her
backside. She started stacking empty plates one atop another.

"Don't you want to eat more? The dishes can wait."

She looked back at Max's warm smile. He seemed like
such a kind man. Still, where had be been when Ryder
needed him in high school?

"That's okay. I guess I'm not very hungry this morning." The truth was Jenny's clothes left little room to
breathe, let alone eat. Now she knew why her friend had
insisted on separate boxes for her loaners. Jenny knew
Essie would never wear them unless she had no choice. As
she piled on another dirty plate, she wondered when the
little vixen had made the box switch.

Remembering where she was, she glanced around the
table and caught Shane's steady gaze. Was he trying to read
her mind, or what?

This one would be hard to fool.

Her breath hitched at the back of her throat as she realized what this last thought meant. She wasn't leaving after

all. She piled on more dishes and exhaled. She'd come this far, why not give it a whirl? If for no other reason than to satisfy her curiosity. Who were these men she'd heard so much about? And Ryder! To think she'd held up this man as the standard for all others! How could she have been so wrong about him?

She made her way around the table and avoided Ryder's face...as if he remembered she was even there. Except for the casual toast toss, he'd all but ignored her. She looked at Joshua, instead, who was spreading jelly...uh, preserves...and giving her a sympathetic smile. She gave him a small smile back, till suddenly she felt the muscles in her arms quiver from her load. Before she could make a fool of herself and drop the whole pile, she pushed open the kitchen door with her back and deposited the dishes next to the sink. Hannah went about her business, not looking up. Essie watched her a moment, then left for another load, mentally sizing up her situation.

Two friendly faces, one questionable, one crude, and one crusty old lady who she'd bet her bottom dollar had a soft side.

Essie filled her arms again and returned to the kitchen, deciding once and for all that she would stay and make the best of things. She'd come to Montana for another look at Ryder Malone. One bad first impression didn't come close to answering all the questions she had about this man. Why, after all these years, was that large chip still on his broad shoulders? She stopped and stared out the back window at a pair of mountains aglow with the morning sun. And how could anyone be unhappy in a paradise such as this?

Before she could change her mind, she marched back into the dining room and stood next to Max. ''If the offer's still open, I'll take it,'' she said, watching the surprise register on his face.

With a wide smile, he pushed out his chair and grasped her hand in both of his. ''We're happy to have you, Essie. Would you like to see your room? You will stay here, won't you?''

She looked around the table one last time. Shane's face told her nothing, Joshua looked like someone just bought him a puppy, and Ryder was still shoveling it in, acting as though he hadn't heard the question, or if he had, didn't care. All the way out here, she'd prayed he wouldn't recognize her. Now that he didn't and the initial disappointment at his behavior had subsided, she wanted to whop him upside the head with a two-by-four.

She squared her shoulders and faced Max. "Yes, sir. I would. I'd love to stay here."

Max patted her shoulder and heaved a sigh. "Great, Essie. Let me show you around."

That was a first, Essie thought, leaving Max at the front door and heading for her car. In Detroit, she'd haggled over every merit raise, as if each nickel would make a difference. Here, she'd accepted a job without knowing how much it would pay, exactly what her duties or hours would be or even what her accommodation would look like.

She started down the bark walkway thinking her instincts had been right. The room had turned out to be a cozy little suite—a bedroom, a sitting room with a fireplace and her own bathroom. It meant the wages were lower than what she was used to, but what would she need money for out here in the wilderness? She paused and turned back to the log house that would soon be her home. Over the roof line she could see the matching pair of mountains she'd spotted earlier. She wondered how far away they were. They seemed close, yet...

"We call 'em the MoJoes."

Startled, she swung around and saw Ryder, squatted behind the hand-carved sign she'd noticed earlier at the end of the walkway. He was toweling it off, of all things, fingering all the grooves. She took her time closing the distance between them, afraid what she might encounter this time.

"Mo, because we think they look like giant molars." He

continued cleaning the grooves, not looking at her. "And Joe, since they overlook the fair city of Joeville."

Essie stopped alongside Ryder and read the oval crest. Arched across the top were the words "The Montana Malones." In the center was carved a beautiful replica of the snow-crested MoJoes, their reflections mirrored in the painted blue waters below. At the bottom of the sign were the words "Joeville, Montana, founded 1876." She wasn't sure she was ready to engage this man in conversation, but since he had started, she trod softly.

"How did this area ever come to be named Joeville?"

Ryder eyed her before answering, then returned to his task. "My great-granddaddy's name was Joe. He was the first to settle here and start the ranch." He chuckled. "In school I got the idea to change it to Joe, Montana." A small smile lifted one corner of his mouth. "Never made it official, but that's what we call it now."

Essie watched the sun play on his handsome face and remembered all those Friday-night football games. Without thinking, she asked, "Do you still throw a ball around…or go to any games?" She saw his face go rigid and, instantly, she realized her mistake. He looked at her sideways, the question taking shape behind his dark eyes before his lips ever moved.

"How did you know I played ball?"

She picked up a stone and skipped it across the small pond in the front yard, giving her heart a chance to beat again. "The trophy case in your dad's study. I just got the tour, remember?"

Ryder pushed off his knees and beat more dust from his jeans. Out of the corner of her eye she could see he was no longer studying her. Now he seemed lost in another time and place.

"Yeah, trophies. He likes to collect 'em. Since he was never there, guess that's all he has." He ran his fingers through his hair, repositioned his hat low on his forehead, turned and walked to his pickup.

Damn. She hadn't meant to awaken that demon. But

why, if they lived under the same roof for all these years, hadn't he and his father come to terms? With one hand on the door handle and the other holding his sunglasses, Ryder looked back at her and her chest constricted again.

"Guess I'll be seeing you around, then…uh, what did you say your name was?"

She met his even stare, wondering if he truly didn't remember her name or if this was another of his games. She imagined he played many. "Essie. Essie Smith." She leaned a little heavy on her last name, watching to see if it triggered anything.

If it did, he masked it well. With his gaze still on hers, he slid his glasses in place and lowered the brim of his hat another notch. "See ya around, Essie Smith."

His tone and grin were suggestive, leaving her breathless and angry, all at the same time. After the slightest pause, he hopped into his pickup, backed it into a stone-throwing arc, and tore down the road the way he'd come.

Two

Less than an hour after he'd arrived, Ryder drove away from the Purple Palace, eyeing it through a veil of dust in the rearview mirror, worrying again about Billy. The months ahead would be difficult, but somehow Ryder would find a way to ease the little guy's fears. At last a plan had been put into motion that should help. At least he hoped it would—if mother nature and the attorneys didn't ruin things before they started.

When he passed under the Malone arch, he put that problem aside and thought of another. In the month since his return home, he still hadn't found his place in the scheme of things. He wanted to help Shane and Josh, but they'd each carved out their own niches, leaving him little but the scraps of daily errands. In part that came in handy, since Maddy and Billy needed him more than ever these days. Yet he missed the comfort of routine.

At the ranch in Helena, where he'd spent most of his adult years, he'd always known how he would spend his days. He had complete charge of the cattle and horses. It was a place where men looked up to him for direction, and women tried to compete with his dim memory of a young girl—a girl he'd thought was his only true friend. Oh, some of the women had succeeded in distracting him short-term. They'd strutted their stuff and he'd danced their dance. For a while. But something was always missing.

Ryder parked his pickup near the stables and headed directly for the corral beyond, the memory of this morning's new cook niggling at a corner of his memory. There was a vague familiarity in the way she talked, or was it the sound of her voice? He couldn't quite get a handle on it. Still...she didn't look like anyone he'd ever met, either in Helena or Joeville.

Shane spotted him and waved his hat high above his head. Old Bucking Horse stood nearby, but he didn't look up. Ryder sauntered toward them, knowing the old Crow heard him approaching. He heard everything, yet said little. Not exactly a fault in Ryder's book, since he was a man of few words himself. He hitched his elbows up onto the fence and scraped the bottom of a boot on a lower rung.

Shane made his way over, running his fingers through his nearly black hair, then resettling his hat in place. "Looking for something to do?"

Yeah, something permanent that he could call his own, he thought, but he didn't say it. He would wait. In time he would find his place. He pushed his hat back on his forehead. "Sure. What do you have?"

"We'll be moving the cattle to summer pasture in a couple weeks. Could use some help on the fence out there. Got a few downed rails." When Ryder didn't jump on that one, Shane offered another. "Or you can help Josh with the Cat. He's about ready to dig irrigation ditches for the hay, but the equipment's been acting up."

"I'll give Josh a hand first, then see to the fence." He scraped off his other boot and looked off at Buck working a horse around the ring. "There's some new quarter horses up for bid in Billings. I was thinking of driving over tomorrow for a look...unless you want to handle it yourself."

Shane regarded him for a moment, then turned his back to the rail and hooked his elbows over the side. "Nah. You go ahead. If you find anything, we could use about four."

Ryder knew the significance of Shane's trust. Horses were his first love—his and Buck's. In the tradition of the Crow tribe, Buck knew his horses, and he'd always shared his vast knowledge with Shane. Their special bond had angered Ryder when he was a kid. Now he understood it was envy, not anger. Buck was the dad Shane had needed at the time. At least his brother had found someone.

Ryder studied Shane's rugged profile, noticing the deep lines at the corner of his eye etched against wind-and-sun-browned skin. He closed his eyes and tilted his high cheekbones to the sun, looking as untroubled as ever. He was seven years Joshua's senior and only three, Ryder's. Ryder looked at his boots and turned over a few stones. Maybe if he'd been the mature son like Shane, instead of the rebellious teenager, he could have stayed at the ranch, too. Detroit may as well have been Siberia, except for that special friend of his....

"Well..." Shane pushed off the fence. "If we're going to get anything done, we can't stand around here working on our tan." He started to walk away, then stopped. "By the way, what do you think of the new cook?"

Ryder flashed him his best bad-boy smile. "Many fine attributes...but I'm sure you noticed."

"Yeah, I noticed. I also noticed she couldn't keep her eyes off you."

"Really?" This was news to him. If anything, he thought he sensed an air of hostility.

"Probably wouldn't help any to encourage her, now would it?" Shane leveled a stern look on him that reminded him of their father, a look that set his teeth on edge.

"I think I'm old enough to handle my own affairs, bro." He turned and walked toward the equipment barn, but he heard Shane's muttered response behind him.

"Yeah, we've all heard about your affairs, little brother. Just don't make this one another."

* * *

The business of repacking her Pontiac at the motel took no time at all. Except for the two suitcases she used last night, the rest of her belongings were still bunched snugly in the trunk of her car. She'd cut the tape on the boxes, looking for the ones that held her own clothes, but since she'd found none, she'd felt no need to drag them into Big Beak Motel. Fortunately she had a few of her things in her suitcases—nightshirts, underwear, shoes and her favorite Michigan sweatshirt.

Essie eyed the Michigan logo a moment before closing the lid. So far she'd avoided mention of her home state. If she wore the sweatshirt, the questions would surely come. She could always say it was a gift from her best friend, Jenny, who went to school there. After all, it was true. Yes. That's exactly what she'd do if the need arose.

She took her time placing the bags in her car before ambling down to the office and paying her bill.

"Leavin' already?" The clerk with the missing teeth showed no sign of vanity as he smiled broadly at her.

"I got a job in Joeville." She looked around his tacky office. Dusty animal heads of every variety covered the dark paneled walls. The ranch was definitely a step up, way up, though she'd miss this old geezer. He'd made her feel right at home from the second she'd signed in.

"Joeville!" His tired eyes widened. He suddenly seemed concerned. "Hope ya mean at the Malone place."

"Yep. That's the place." She pocketed her receipt and watched his worry lines relax. "Why? Is there another?"

"Well...uh, well, there's the Purple Palace." He gave her a dismissive wave. "I was sure ya didn't mean there." He kept his head down, busying himself with mail. "You'll be real happy at the Malones'." He looked up and flashed her another smile.

She thought about asking him about this Purple Palace, but she was eager to begin her journey. She walked to her car, feeling a little awkward for leaving, as if she were abandoning this lonely guy for greener pastures, which was exactly what she was doing.

He shouted after her. "Stop by and say howdy if ya ever nearby."

She waved back at him and kept moving. "I will." She got into her car and drove off, her mood an odd mix of sadness and excitement. She'd only spent two nights at Big Beak, but the old guy acted as though she were family, a trait she'd noticed often the farther west she'd traveled. Out here people looked her in the eye and seemed to care when they said hello. There was no rush, no harried business that couldn't wait. So unlike Detroit. Not that she didn't like Detroit, she admonished herself. Its pulse kept her moving, working, searching....

Another mile and Essie edged off the highway and killed the ignition, a little rattled by her last thought.

Searching? Now where did that come from? She let the word tumble and churn awhile, testing its validity. She stared through the gritty windshield, then finally expelled a long breath. Yes, it was true. All her life she'd been searching, not just for another Ryder Malone, as foolish as that seemed now, but for something far more important. And now here, in this ranging wilderness, she felt certain she knew what that something was.

Peace of mind.

As though emerging from a dream, she stepped from her car and took in the endless blue sky, an eerie awareness seeping into her.

Jenny had been right. She was never going back.

Even though the noonday sun shimmered heat waves off the asphalt, Essie hugged herself and shivered. The vastness of the sky and rolling planes gobbled her up, making her one with it. Through the bottoms of her thin-soled sandals, she felt the pebbled earth beneath her, its depth and firmness coalescing, already sprouting the roots she'd subconsciously sought.

She'd never felt so at peace.

Somehow she placed herself behind the wheel of her car and continued on. She'd driven this road only this morning, but then she'd been nervous, filled with apprehension and anxiety, afraid what might happen when she saw Ryder after all these years. She was still afraid, mostly that time would change nothing, that he would never be the man she'd dreamed of. Yet she knew it was too soon for such thoughts. If she'd lived through twelve years of fantasies, certainly he was worth twelve weeks of observation. After that, or before if need be, she would find a place of her own. But one thing was indisputable: Ryder or no Ryder, Montana would forever be her home. How she knew this with such certainty, or how Jenny had known it before, seemed insignificant.

It was true.

She backed off the accelerator and studied the vista, familiarizing herself with her new home, growing more comfortable with each passing mile of wildflowers. Somewhere in the recesses of her mind, she was aware of the deception that lay ahead—not just the times when she would actually have to prepare meals, but, worse, when she would have to face Ryder with her true identity. She tucked these worries away, determined to enjoy the moment. *Carpe diem.* When was the last time she'd seized the day? She couldn't remember. Smiling, she drove on.

At long last she knew the source of Ryder's wistful smile—the one she'd remembered so long ago whenever he spoke of home, and the generations of Malones who worked and loved this God-touched wilderness. The closer she got to the ranch, the more she felt the pieces of his heritage seep into her, and she knew her decision to stay had been the right one.

Just as she had planned, Hannah had things well in hand for supper by the time Essie had moved the last box from her car to her new digs upstairs and then strolled into the kitchen.

Hannah threw her a derisive glance, then went about her business. "Nice of ya ta stop by," she said, whacking at a helpless onion, wiping her red eyes on her sweat-stained sleeve.

Essie smiled and ignored the sarcasm, still enjoying the glow of her drive in. "What would you like me to help with?"

"Help?" Hannah nearly shouted. "This here is *yer* job. I'm supposed ta be doin' other things."

Essie felt her heart sink to her growling stomach. As gruff as this old lady was, Essie much preferred the idea of being her helper than head chef.

"I—I'm sorry I'm so late. Maybe I can help you with your chores when we're done here." She cast a hopeful glance in the woman's direction.

"Humph." She continued taking out her vengeance on the poor onion.

It was then Essie noticed the large mixing bowl of ground beef. She had a sinking suspicion one of her few good meals was about to be scratched from this week's list. "Meat loaf?" she asked, hoping against hope she was wrong.

"'Less ya got somethin' else in mind."

"N-no. Meat loaf's fine."

"Good. Then ya kin work on the scalloped potatoes."

Without a box? She looked around for a clue as to where to start.

"Taters are in the wood bin...end o' counter." Hannah nodded with her head while she used the side of her knife to scrape diced onions into the mixing bowl.

Essie found the bin and retrieved twelve large potatoes, taking them to the sink to peel.

"Which ones cain't eat?" Hannah barked over her shoulder.

"Not enough?" Essie darted back to the bin, feeling about as out of place as Jenny would in front of a computer. Damn her ideas, anyway. How could a person pull out a cookbook with Hannah the Horrible breathing down her neck? The idea of making scalloped potatoes from scratch was as alien as butchering her own meat. Oh, God. Would she have to do that, too?

"Try doublin' that and ya'll be close."

Essie toted another dozen to the sink, found the right utensil in a half-opened drawer, and went to work under a running faucet.

"Don't know where ya from, but we all conserve water 'round here. Fill the sink, if ya have ta, but turn off that tap."

Essie did as she was told, keeping her face forward to hide the anger and embarrassment that was coloring her cheeks. As much as she dreaded the thought of solo kitchen duty, the sooner this woman was in another part of the house, the better.

She could feel Hannah's critical eyes boring into her back, and she double-timed the potato peeler, venting her frustrations while hoping to appear as if she knew what she was doing. At least Ryder was nowhere in sight to witness this impending disaster.

The screen door squeaked, then banged shut behind heavy boots thudding across the wooden plank floor. The boots stopped, and Essie kept peeling, head down, praying it was anyone other than Ryder.

"How's it going, Hannah?"

Great. The familiar voice tightened the knot in Essie's stomach.

"Ma bunions are killin' me, but that ain't nothin' new," Hannah said, with a half chuckle.

Essie peeled and prayed. *Please make him go away. I've got enough on my hands.*

"Whatcha been up ta all day, young Ryder?" Hannah practically purred, her voice taking on a dulcet tone.

"Oh, a little of this, less of that."

"Shane tells me ya goin' to Billings to look at some quarter horses t'morrow."

"Yep. Need something?"

This brought Essie's head around. She didn't want Ryder to go grocery shopping. She had to do it. Alone.

Ryder looked her way, touched the brim of his hat and nodded. "Evening, Essie." He was looking at what she wore, his gaze never quite making it to her eyes.

"Hello," she said tightly, then turned back to her chore, angry with him for his lecherous leering, more angry with herself for still caring.

"The pantry's runnin' low, but I'm sure ya'd rather not go a-shoppin'." Hannah actually laughed. There was no sound of rebuke in her voice, but instead, a fond tolerance. "You make a list and I'll get whatever your big heart desires."

Essie swallowed a chuckle, not believing the exchange behind her. Manure was in abundance in these parts, she reminded herself. Obviously it had found its way from the bottom of his boots to his tongue.

"Maybe Essie should go with ya...show'er where ta go and all."

No! Bad idea. How could she buy boxed mixes and all the other shortcuts she'd decided on, and—

"Fine by me," Ryder said. "What do you think, Essie? You're pretty quiet back there."

I think I'm out of my mind. She turned to meet his gaze, but his focus was somewhere in the vicinity of her backside. She pretended not to notice. "If you have other business, maybe I should go alone...then it won't take all day." His head came up and he finally met her glare.

Hannah's fingers kneaded the ingredients in the bowl and missed the exchange. "Y'all go ahead. What's one more day? Ya have ta learn yer way 'round sooner or later, girl. Might as well be sooner."

Essie watched the woman's sure hands grease a couple of long bread pans, then divide the meat in two, preferring this view to anything she might find on Ryder's face.

Without breaking stride, and acting as though the previous discussion was settled, Hannah spoke to Ryder, her shoulders rolling with her work. "Have ya got a date yet?"

Date? Essie turned back to the sink, feeling a choke hold on her windpipe. Behind her, she heard Ryder sigh and plant his elbows on the counter near Hannah.

"Any chance you'll let me off the hook on this one?" he asked, not sounding too put out.

"Now what would a birthday party be without a date?"

"Don't you think I'm a little old for a birthday party?"

"Humph. When yer my age, talk ta me 'bout old."

Ryder laughed easily. "Okay, okay. As long as you promise…no pointy hats or horns or the like."

"Good. That's settled. Now who ya gonna ask?"

"I was thinking about asking Maddy and her son, Billy."

"Maddy…Maddy. Now where do I know that name from? Don't spect ya met her at church." Ryder laughed and she tried again. "She one of them divorcees, then?"

"More like widowed, I'd say." Then quickly he changed the subject. "Billy's young, but he won't be any problem. Very well-behaved kid."

"Humph."

Essie quickened the stroke on her peeler. Why should she care? Ryder was not the man she'd hoped to find, and she was probably deluding herself to hope otherwise. Let Maddy, or the rest of Montana, have him. She dropped a skinned potato into the water and found another fresh one, the sudden tightness in her chest calling her a liar.

Damn it, anyway. Why couldn't she forget that melancholy young man she had known so well in Detroit? Was he anywhere to be found under all those layers of dust and anger? Her hands stopped. Or was it a moot point? Maybe this Maddy was the reason for the rumpled clothes and the mid-breakfast arrival this morning. And what about Billy? Could he be Ryder's? No. She was letting her imagination run away with her.

"Well," Ryder began, then yawned loudly, as if she needed to be reminded he probably hadn't slept all night, "I got work to do. Better get a move on."

Essie heard his boots inching closer and she stiffened. Then she heard him plant a noisy kiss on Hannah's cheek, which elicited a girlish giggle from the woman.

"Get outta here," she said, lightheartedly.

"See you two ladies at supper." The boots clomped to the back door, and the screen slammed shut behind him.

Essie breathed a sigh of relief. Supper was enough to

manage without the likes of Ryder Malone lurking around. She eyed the last potato in her hands and forced herself to forget him, at least for now. Later she'd analyze the thudding in her ears and the irregular beat of her heart. Right now she had a job to do.

The next step was slicing, but beyond that she hadn't a clue. She needed to run upstairs and look at her cookbook. If she didn't get Hannah out of here soon, she'd be in a world of trouble.

"Hannah," she started tentatively, then rushed on before the woman could stop her. "Why don't you let me finish up here. I know you have other work." Behind her she heard balls of meat being pounded into submission inside baking pans.

"There. Them are ready."

Essie braved a backward glance. Hannah was untying her apron. A good sign.

"Okay, girl. It's all yers." She stopped and looked at her squarely, as if estimating the risk she was taking if she left the task in the rookie's hands. Then she turned and waddled toward the hallway. "The men like ta eat at six sharp."

The second she was out of sight, Essie dried her hands and ran up the back stairs to her room. A few minutes later, with instructions scribbled on a scrap of paper, she tucked it in the pocket of her jeans and darted back to the kitchen, grateful it was still empty. Breathing heavily, she reread the directions, cursed Jenny under her breath and went to work.

At suppertime the four men sat around the table in stony silence, their forks moving from their plates to their mouths slowly, heads bent. Essie moved around the table refilling iced tea glasses, wishing someone would say something. Everything looked pretty good, if she did say so herself. She'd found enough leftover rolls to warm in the microwave. The peas had been easy enough. There were a few lumps of flour in the scalloped potatoes, but beyond that, she thought she'd fared well for her first performance. Max glanced at her over his tea, and she smiled at him, feeling proud. He set his glass down and smiled back, but didn't speak.

She returned to the kitchen and dropped onto one of the chairs at the square little table in the corner facing a cozy bay window and a perfect view of the MoJoes. She stared at the mountains a moment, then down at the two plates she'd set out for Hannah and herself, debating whether she should wait for her companion. Before she had time to decide, Hannah ambled in, looking older and more stooped than before. For a moment Essie forgot the woman's gruffness and felt a pang of empathy. She was too old for all this work. Her eyelids drooped as heavily as her shoulders.

Without benefit of a single word, Hannah scooped potatoes and peas onto her plate, sliced off some meat loaf and dropped a roll in the only clean spot left. Silently she bowed her head a moment, then began to shovel it in like there was no tomorrow.

Essie watched and waited from the opposite side of the table, but Hannah never slowed her pace or lifted her eyes. Maybe this was how they ate out here, Essie thought. All the fresh air and hard work made for a healthy appetite. Words could wait. She went about filling her own plate, eager to taste the fruits of her labor. She blew on a forkful of potatoes and then slid it into her mouth, closing her eyes, ready to savor her masterpiece.

Her teeth, which refused to meet in the middle, discovered the first problem. The potatoes were as hard as granite, almost raw. She persevered, chewed hard and swallowed.

Next was the meat loaf. Hannah had made it; at least *it* had to be good. Except when she cut into the center it almost mooed at her. She ate around the edges and reached for a roll and a dab of butter. The knife sawed back and forth but wouldn't penetrate the crust. The blade must be dull, she concluded. She bit into it, instead. With her lips attached to one side of it, she eyed Hannah's abandoned roll at the edge of her plate and saw teeth marks. Now how could this be? She'd tasted a cold one before warming them. They seemed fine. She'd even left them in the microwave a couple of extra minutes to be sure they were heated through.

Essie ate some peas, not sure if they'd passed the test, either. Canned tasted so much different, she wasn't sure. They were hot and not too hard and Hannah had finished all of hers and was reaching for a second helping.

"Them peas are just right," she said, making fleeting eye contact. "Taters are tasty. Jes need another half hour or so in the oven. Spect there'll be plenty a' leftovers. Be jes right next time."

Essie could feel the moisture on her bottom lashes. She blinked furiously, feeling an enormous gratitude. She'd blown it. Hannah knew it, but didn't issue the tongue-lashing she deserved. Essie's appraisal of this woman this morning had already proven true. There *was* a marshmallow under all those dimples and rolls...and a degree of sensitivity that surprised and touched her.

"Did ya make dessert?" Hannah ate the edges around another slice of meat loaf and Essie dropped her fork on her plate.

She sighed in defeat. Out of the corner of her eye she could see Hannah's hand stop midair and felt the woman's weary stare.

"Ice cream's in the freezer on the porch. Got some berries in the fridge...if ya wanna pour some over."

Essie looked up, hoping the tears wouldn't spill and she wouldn't make a fool of herself. But Hannah was tackling another mouthful of potatoes, head down.

"Thank you," Essie said, and went to the freezer.

When she entered the dining room with her tray of four bowls, the men were busily engaged in a discussion about quarter horses and didn't stop when she took their unfinished plates and replaced them with the ice cream.

As she pushed her back against the door to the kitchen, Ryder's gaze locked on her face and she felt the color drain from it.

"Pick you up at the kitchen door in the morning. How's eight o'clock?"

"F-fine." She averted her eyes and carried her load to the kitchen. Behind her she heard a burst of laughter and could only imagine what was being said about supper and the new cook. She started rinsing and stacking dirty dishes, glad her back was to Hannah and whomever else might walk through.

Oh, Jenny. How I wish you were here.

She paused and looked out the window. The sun was low in the sky, casting a reddish glow over the mountains. Even though it was early June, snow still blanketed the upper ridges, while fields of wildflowers stretched the distance between here and there, a cool evening breeze tilting their colorful heads eastward. A modicum of the peace she felt earlier returned. Montana was a sight to behold. There was no doubt she'd remain in this paradise, but how long would she survive under this roof? Already they knew her credentials were shaky. When would they ask her to leave?

But of more immediate concern was how she would handle tomorrow with Ryder...alone in the close confines of his truck.

Three

"**J**es as I spected! She don't know squat 'bout cookin'."

Max crossed his arms over his chest and frowned. "Last night was her first night. Maybe she was just nervous. It's not like we have dozens of applicants to choose from, Hannah. You can't continue doing it all yourself—"

"So that's why I decided I'd have ta teach her," she said, interrupting him.

Max's chin dropped. Before he could recover, Essie walked down the back stairs, her eyes bloodshot and red rimmed.

When she spotted the pair, she stopped on the last step and took in their smiling faces. Smiles? They were the last things she expected to find this morning. And why was Hannah in the kitchen instead of doing her housework?

"Good morning, Essie," Max said, his smile still fixed in place.

"Good morning, Mr. Malone."

"Max. Please."

She stepped into the kitchen, not sure what to expect

next. "Max," she repeated, and braved a look at Hannah. "Morning, Hannah."

"Mornin'." She rubbed her hands together, then said, "Maxwell? If y'all will scuse us, we got breakfast ta get on the table."

Max did a mock salute and left the room. Hannah banged a couple of skillets on top of burners, turned up the heat, then began unloading food from the refrigerator to the center counter chopping block.

"Well, don't jes stand there with yer mouth hangin' open. Put on yer apron and let's get ta work."

Breakfast was a huge success, thanks to Hannah's tutelage. Essie only wished the conversation could have gone as smoothly. Unfortunately Hannah had one thing on her mind this morning: Ryder's birthday party on Saturday. If the remarks had been limited to the menu, Essie would have begun to relax. It was the rest of it that had her stomach in knots again: "It's 'bout time he settled down…maybe this Maddy is jes the right woman for Ryder…he seems ta like the li'l boy…if he's the one I seen 'im with a couple times out back."

By the time Essie finally climbed into the passenger's seat of Ryder's pickup, she'd decided on a little harmless probing. The drive to Billings would take over an hour. Plenty of time to find out how important this Maddy was to him. She'd bide her time, though, and let the conversation take its natural course.

The farther northeast they traveled, the darker the clouds that hung heavy in the sky, looking as though their loads were about to burst. Country music blasted from the dashboard making conversation difficult—which was exactly the way Ryder liked it. When thunder began rumbling, and lightning sliced through the darkness, he saw Essie reach for the knob and turn the volume down.

"Don't like country?" He shot her a superior smirk, expecting a negative response.

"Country's fine." Her voice was even, with only a hint

of annoyance. "It was just too loud for me." Then she made the mistake of looking in his direction. He stared at her fire engine red knit top.

"I'd have to disagree," he said, lifting his gaze to hers. "Looks like you *love* loud...not to mention you wear it well."

She jerked her attention back to the windshield as the first drops of rain fell. Her chest rose and fell, and he could see her anger building just below the surface. He decided not to push further. They had a long day ahead of them.

The storm outside was a lazy one, with gentle claps and flashes growing more distant behind mountains to the south, providing a cozy sense of security in the small, dry cab of the truck.

After a while he said, "Breakfast was great this morning." He looked over and saw a small smile tilt a corner of her mouth. "Must be Hannah made it, huh?"

Her smile disappeared as quickly as it came. "Most of it, yes. Thanks for mentioning it."

He shook his head and gave in to a low grumble of laughter. "Essie, that debut supper was something else."

She crossed her legs and started tapping the top one in time to the music. Maybe he should back off a little. Then again, she seemed so easy to tease.

"Can't wait to see the show Saturday night. Is Hannah gonna let you in the kitchen with guests at the table?" He slapped the steering wheel and laughed louder.

"So you want to impress Maddy, do you?"

He stole a sideways glance and felt his smile slip a notch. Her scowl had been replaced with an arched eyebrow and a curious smile.

"I'd like Maddy to have a good time. She deserves that much...and so does her son, Billy."

She hiked one leg under her, leaned her left shoulder into the back of the seat and tilted her head. "You seem to like this Billy."

Whatever accounted for her shift in mood, he decided to play along. "Yeah. Billy's a neat kid...seven goin' on seventeen. Thinks of himself as the man of the house." A vice tightened around his heart and the rest came out in a rush. "Which he is...since his dad took off before he was born."

When she didn't ask more on the subject, a silence as thick as the humidity permeating the interior of the truck hung between them.

After a while he wondered why he was giving Essie such a hard time. Being new to the ranch had to be difficult enough for her. He doubted she'd lived long in Montana, either. She didn't sound anything like a Westerner. With his arm draped over the steering wheel, he kept his eyes on the road and decided to find out.

"Sounds to me like you're from the Midwest somewhere."

There was a long pause, and he was about to repeat the question when she said, "Yes, I lived in the Midwest for a while." In what sounded like a forced lightness, she added, "But I've always wanted to live in Montana...and now here I am."

She was hiding something and he was suddenly curious what. "Why Montana?"

"M-my best friend in high school was from here...told me great stories...always made it sound beautiful."

He glanced at her briefly, then back to the rain pelting the window. "Best friend...hmm. I had one of those once upon a time. Yep. A very special lady, she was." Out of the corner of his eye, he saw her stop swinging her leg. When she didn't offer more, he probed further. "Have you seen this best friend of yours since you moved west?"

She recrossed her legs in the opposite direction and faced the side window. "We sort of lost contact."

"Yeah, well, I know how that goes. We did, too."

Essie said nothing, the silence stretching uncomfortably.

"Guess it was for the best in my case. She probably realized I'm not exactly the letter-writing kind, anyway." He might have written, though, had they not had that incident just before he left Detroit. He could still see the pained expression on Savannah's face when she'd caught him necking with another girl after the senior prom. For a while he'd thought it might be easier to let her assume the worst since he would be leaving town soon, but later when he tried to explain it was the floozy who had come on to him, Savannah wouldn't even talk to him. And so he'd left town, feeling bruised and confused. Just about the way he'd felt when he'd arrived.

Ryder tugged at his Stetson and straightened in his seat, trying to shelve what should have been ancient history. "You know, that whole thing taught me a valuable lesson." He noticed she was eyeing the cluster of buildings straight ahead, acting as though she wished they were there already. "Yep. Taught me never to lose my head over a woman. Having a little fun is one thing, but caring too much causes nothing but problems and—"

"Is that Billings up there?" she interrupted, sending a clear signal she'd had enough of his opinions regarding women.

"Yeah, sure is." The rain had slowed to a drizzle, and a rainbow arced over the city and the wilderness far beyond.

"Do you ever get used to this?" She pressed forward against her seat belt for a better view of the massive cloud-tufted sky. "What's your favorite part about Montana?" she asked, before he could answer her first question.

Through her side of the truck he spotted a lone moose grazing in the distance and nodded for her to look. No walls or fence confined his foraging. Acres of unspoiled land welcomed his freedom. By the expression on Essie's face, he'd bet his bottom dollar she'd never seen such creatures outside of a zoo.

"Wow. Look at that," she said in a hushed tone. "Can you imagine carrying around a rack like that all the time?" She looked over her shoulder at him.

With his focus below her shoulders, he smiled. "You'd be a better judge of that." He knew he was intentionally baiting her and he didn't know why. She crossed her arms below her breasts, which only served to exaggerate her generous cleavage. When he snickered she glared back at him.

"Oh, for Pete's sake. You have a one-track mind."

"Not true. Savannahs," he said, then laughed again.

Essie's eyes widened. "What?"

"Savannahs," he repeated, puzzled by her reaction. "See? I *can* think of two things at once. You asked me what's my favorite part about Montana, so I'm telling you."

Essie released a long breath and leaned back.

"I've always loved it all," he said, noticing red blotches on her neck, pretending he hadn't. "But the part that surprised me, that I never thought I'd love as much, was the sight of a savannah at sunset."

Essie turned her face to the passing moose.

"People think of mountains and streams and trees when they think of beauty. Yet there's something truly awesome about savannahs—or the plains—areas where the sky touches the earth for miles on end. There's no place but the sea where you'll find such vastness."

She didn't respond, which was fine with him. Whatever her game, he figured he would hear about it sooner or later. Another thing he'd learned about women—they weren't very good with secrets. And this gorgeous lady definitely harbored a secret. It was obvious she couldn't cook, that she'd lied to get the job. But he sensed there was more. Much more. She seemed to watch him like a hawk, yet he couldn't say she was flirting with him. If anything, she seemed annoyed whenever he flirted with her. And if she were simply after a man, then why not Shane or Josh? She barely looked their way when he was around.

And most disturbing of all, why did he still have this vague sense of meeting her before?

Essie sank lower in her seat, lost in the image he'd painted with his whiskey, morning voice. *This* was the man she'd fallen in love with more than a dozen years ago. *This* was the man she had hoped to find again—the one with the poetic soul. She rested her head against the seat and closed her eyes.

Ryder Malone—*her* Ryder Malone—was still alive and kicking. She didn't know whether to celebrate or cry— celebrate because he still possessed a spot of sensitivity for the world around him, or cry because another woman had meant so much to him to have caused him pain. Who was this special woman he referred to? She'd wanted to ask, but she was afraid what she might hear. By the way he'd said it, it hadn't sounded as though it were Maddy. But then who? In the dozen years since she'd seen him, she knew there had to be at least one special person in his life, yet sharing the details was more than she was prepared for, though she was curious what happened to cause such bitterness. Still, whatever it was, she doubted it justified his attitude toward all women, or life in general.

Why was he like this? she wondered, looking through narrowed slits at his long, jeans-clad legs. Somehow she'd thought he would be different by now. And why, after all these years, hadn't he reconciled with his father? In the brief time she'd seen them together, she'd felt their discomfort with each other. There was so much she didn't know about this family, especially this older Ryder.

With her heart beating to the rhythm of a fast two-step on the radio, they pulled off the highway west of the city, and there she made a silent vow: one way or the other, before she left Joeville for good, she would get to the bottom of what was gnawing at this man beside her.

Watching him barter for quarter horses, tall and confident, in an arena only slightly familiar to her, did nothing to quiet Essie's growing attraction. It reminded her of the few times they'd gone riding in Michigan. Nearly everything she knew about horses came from Ryder. Then, as now, the animals seemed to read his every movement. He'd stop ahead of each in the pen, snapping a rope at a horse's hindquarters when it slowed, making eye contact often. She remembered him teaching her that visual communication was ninety percent of mastering any horse. She watched him another hour with several different ones, proving his point with each.

Once he'd decided which horses he would bid on at the auction later in the week, Ryder shifted the conversation to baling hay. For some reason Essie had thought he just lived off his father's fortune, coming and going as the mood moved him. Actually working the ranch, going as far as helping Josh in baling their own hay for the horses' feed, somehow surprised her. And pleased her. She felt proud of him suddenly, and realized she was treading on dangerous ground.

Essie eyed a small, stocky mare and drifted away from the men, amazed at the depth of Ryder's knowledge and the respect shown to him by the others. She reached into her hip pocket and pulled out a butter mint and offered it to the mare, who took it eagerly as Essie stroked its platinum mane and pretended not to eavesdrop.

"Glad to hear you moved back to your pa's," one of the men said.

Essie's hand stilled on the mare's silky neck, and she glanced over her shoulder. Moved back? She'd assumed he'd lived there all along.

"Yeah, well...guess it was about time," Ryder said, drawing a line in the dirt with the toe of his boot. "Besides, Shane and Josh could use a hand. You probably heard Josh is set on starting a farm."

"Bet your pa's thrilled with that," one of the men said, and the others laughed, rolling their eyes.

"Not exactly. Pure ranchers rarely do." Ryder laughed, too, but Essie caught his sardonic expression.

"Well, be sure ta say howdy for us," another said.

Ryder said he would as he finally approached Essie to leave. He cupped his large hand under one elbow and gently ushered her back to the pickup. It was a light touch, undemanding, its gentleness leaving her little doubt she'd lost the battle of keeping an emotional distance. He even opened her door and boosted her into her seat.

"Can you hand me that towel behind the bench?" he asked.

She leaned over, found it and passed it back to him. From the back window, she watched as he dried a few remaining puddles on the tarp that covered the bed. A few minutes later he hopped behind the wheel and turned the key.

"Ready for the Piggly Wiggly?" He slanted her a smile and her pulse played hopscotch once again.

"Piggly Wiggly?" she said after a moment.

"The supermarket…just up the road." He backed out of the spot without waiting for her answer.

Terrific. How was she supposed to buy all those quick fixes she planned to hide in her room. "Don't you have other errands while you're in town?"

"A few."

"Why don't you drop me off, then meet me back there later?"

He shrugged but didn't look at her. "How much time do you need?"

She pulled the list Hannah had given her from her pocket and scanned down the unfamiliar products. "Is an hour and a half okay?" Still looking at the long list, she wondered if she should have said two hours.

"Wait inside where it's cool. I'll find you." He stopped in front of the store, the engine idling. "Got enough money?"

"Hannah gave me plenty," she said, patting her purse and stepping out onto the sidewalk.

He tipped his hat, then looked down at her cleavage and chuckled. "See you later, then." The pickup screeched away, leaving her at the curb with her face as red as her knit top.

At mealtime that night, Ryder looked up whenever Essie entered the dining room, meeting her eyes every time. Always, she looked away first, busying herself with platters, refilling iced tea glasses, pretending he wasn't there. Just the way she had when they'd driven home.

Most of the way back she'd curled on her side, leaned into the seat and feigned sleep. Although, often when he'd looked over, he'd caught her eyelids slamming shut. Then, as now, he wondered what she was up to.

The setting sun streaked through the bay window, enhancing the sheen of her dark, silky hair. He wondered if it felt as soft as it looked. Her full lips were glossy and peach tinted. And so inviting. She rushed past him, and he got a light whiff of coconut, a vague sense of familiarity niggling at him again. Was it her shampoo or perfume? Whatever it was, he liked it.

Not smart, guy, he lectured himself. A fling with the hired help would only complicate things. How would he keep away from her when it ended? Would she leave Hannah in the lurch if her feelings got hurt? He watched her push the kitchen door open with her back and leave the room again. She acted tough, talked tough, but no doubt about it—this one had feelings, the kind that got hurt. Still, she also had a little of that come-hither look. Why else would she be studying his every move? And wearing those sexy clothes?

"Find any quarter horses you liked?" His father pulled his attention back to the ever-present business at the table.

"Yes. Four or five look especially good." He emptied his glass, hoping Essie would notice when she returned. "I'll take the trailer with me to the auction and hope for the best."

Essie walked behind him and refilled his glass, the coconut scent growing stronger. What was it about that smell that seemed familiar?

"Mind if I tag along next time?" Josh asked. "I'd like to check out a few books from the library."

Max set his fork down with a clang. "Don't tell me you're still toying with those farming ideas?"

"A lot of ranches are diversifying lately," Ryder argued for his younger brother. "It makes good business sense."

Josh shot his brother a look that said he could fight his own battles.

Max looked from one to the other. "This is a ranch. And it's going to stay that way. Ranchers don't grow crops. Farmers do." He resumed eating as though the subject were closed.

"That's why I've been thinking of remodeling grand-dad's old place. It's far enough away from grazing land, and I think I'd like living up there." Josh slid his words out in a quiet fashion, not resorting to Ryder's confrontational tone. Just a simple statement of fact.

From the corner of his eye, Ryder watched his father and waited, but no further words were spoken on the subject. There was little doubt about it: Josh would have his farm, and his father wouldn't fight him in the end. How simple it seemed between the two of them.

How much different it was for the middle son who knew too much about the father Joshua worshiped.

Four

At dusk Wednesday night, Ryder sauntered outside to find Bucking Horse and tell him about the new quarter horses he'd seen. It had been a long time since the two of them had had a good after-dinner cigar and a little powwow. He passed through the stables, checking there first, then walked on to the cabin beyond, where the Indian shared his simple lodgings with Shane. Neither was in sight, so he doubled back, feeling disappointed.

Silhouetted in front of the last stall, he spotted Essie. He stopped and watched her from afar. She was talking softly to a brown and white paint pony, her palm up in front of his nuzzle. Curious, it sniffed and made a soft snorting noise before Essie stepped in and stroked his neck.

Ryder walked toward her, liking what he saw—not just the woman, but her way with the pony. She may not be a Montanan, yet somewhere along the line she'd learned about horses. They sensed her lack of fear, something he'd noticed before when they'd been in Billings. She saw him coming and turned her back to a dividing post, looking startled and suddenly ill at ease. The pony whinnied behind her, sensing her shift in mood.

As Ryder approached he saw her eyes trained on him, and again he wondered what she was afraid of, what she was hiding. He stopped and leaned on the gate, which brought the pony forward in the stall, nudging its nose at Ryder's breast pocket.

"Billy's got you spoiled, little paint," Ryder said, pulling a butter mint from his pocket and letting the horse help itself. He stroked the pony's mane and looked at Essie. "This is Billy's favorite. I've been thinking of giving it to him soon."

"He comes here often?" Essie seemed surprised, and Ryder wondered why it mattered to her.

"Just a few times…here in the stables with me." But not in the house. He'd never wanted to hear the inevitable questions from Hannah about the boy's mother, so they'd stuck to riding and visiting the stables. Come Saturday night that would all be different. He glanced at Essie who had a sad, faraway expression on her face.

"There's a foal at the other end. Would you like to take a peek?" This brought a smile to her lips, which warmed him in an unexpected way. He liked the way her eyes smiled when her lips curved upward.

He turned and walked back to the new mother, a big reddish bay. Essie caught up to him, bringing a rush of coconut-scented air with her. Ryder inhaled deeply. "Let me guess. Shampoo or suntan lotion?"

She looked stumped and simply frowned at him.

"That coconut smell…I noticed it yesterday, too." Again she looked startled. Why was she so jumpy?

"I…uh…it's perfume…a gift from a friend of mine." She turned toward the foal, but not before he saw the pink on her cheeks. "Oh, look. He's trying to get up."

Side by side they watched as the young one uncurled in the corner and struggled to his feet. On tottering stilts, he peered from behind the shelter of his mother, and Essie laughed.

Her gaze stayed fixed on the little one's actions. "He's adorable."

Ryder turned sideways and watched her. When she noticed she blushed again.

"What are you staring at?" she asked.

She tried sounding angry, but he knew it was embarrassment he heard. He could have made it easier for her, but it wasn't his nature. "Just you. Does that bother you?" He knew it did and waited to see what she would say next.

She stepped away from him and pressed her back against a corner post. Her eyes were now on a piece of hay she bent in her fingers. "Why should that bother me?"

He stepped closer and braced his hand above her head. He heard her sharp intake of air. "You tell me." From this vantage point, he could see the swell of her breasts rising and falling. Something didn't fit. Not just her too-small knit top, but more the fact that she would wear such a thing. It didn't seem to match this nervous woman, breathing quicker in front of him and ignoring his question. Part of him said walk away. Now. There was Maddy and Billy to consider. Yet another part wanted to lower his head and press his lips to that soft, exposed swell, to breathe in the coconut scent of her.

He could feel her breath against the open neck of his shirt, and he spoke without thinking. "You know," he said, lifting her chin with his index finger. "You shouldn't be wearing this kind of stuff unless you want this kind of attention." He inched a little closer, his gaze riveted on her full lips. Her tongue moistened them, then darted back inside as if caught doing something wrong. "Or is this exactly what you've been looking for?"

"I haven't been looking for anything." She turned her head to the side, still refusing to meet his eyes.

"Is that right?" His laugh was low and nonbelieving. "Well then, how come every time I look around, I catch you watching me? Or are you one of those women who make a study of men's backsides?"

She pushed him hard with both hands, sending him stag-

gering backward, her eyes finally finding his. Before he
could advance again, he heard Josh call from the house.

"Ryder...Maddy's on the phone."

"Be right there," he called back, then looked at Essie.
She was coiled with her back against the stall, looking like
a rattler poised to strike.

"Well, blue eyes, it'll just have to wait for another day."
He slapped his hat against his leg, slid it back on his head
and walked away.

Every possible derogatory name raced through her mind
and threatened to let loose, but Essie reined in her temper,
along with the sorrel Buck had saddled for her earlier, and
left the stable without a backward glance. The horse's
hooves pounded the hard trail, keeping time with the loud
beat of her heart, neither slowing till she reached the ridge.
Once there she stopped near a clump of overgrown shrub,
where the horse nibbled at branches and Essie slumped in
her saddle and sucked in air.

Her first impression last Monday had been right. Spoiled,
self-centered, arrogant...and now she could add *womanizer*
to the list. Probably anyone with a healthy dose of estrogen
grabbed his attention. And who knows what other parts.
She didn't want to think about it.

But she did. Not just now, but every day since her arrival. Ryder in other women's arms. And now Maddy's.

Yet the prevailing image this very moment was that of
his lips mere inches from her own. All she'd had to do was
lean in a little closer—a simple enough act, one she'd
dreamed of for more than a dozen years.

And she'd blown it.

She looked out over the valley and the red glow of the
setting sun behind the MoJoes. Who was she kidding? It
didn't matter how macho he acted. His tough-guy act didn't
fool her. Beneath that glacial facade she knew a heart beat
strong and good. She could have broken through that ice,
perhaps thawed it a little, if only she had seized the moment. If things never worked out with Ryder, at least she

could have left this place relishing the feel of him, the taste of him. But no, she'd been typically insecure and let the chance slip away. She lifted the horse's reins and kicked her heels, spurring the sorrel back on the trail. Next time, if there was a next time, things would be different.

She pushed the horse to a steady lope, trying to dispel her frustration and confusion. She thought she knew him so well. Except for that awful prom night, the young man in Michigan hadn't even dated. Yet all the clues this week pointed to his being hell-bent on making up for lost time. And then there was this Maddy. Whoever she was, she and her son were important enough to be invited to the birthday party on Saturday. So why had he come on to someone he thought was a stranger back at the stables?

She followed a path down to a stream and stopped to let her horse drink, still thinking about the kiss that could have been. Finally she growled aloud, angry with herself as much as that impossible man. "But don't think for a second, Ryder Malone, that you'll earn another notch on your bedpost from this woman!"

"You tell 'em, Essie!"

She swiveled in the saddle and was shocked to see Shane's smile, his back to a tree trunk, a long shaft of grass between his teeth. She took her time dismounting, facing the other way till the heat left her cheeks. When she turned, Shane stood a yard away, and she fell back against her horse. "You're always doing that!"

"Doing what?"

"You know...staring at me."

His eyes laughed before his lips gave way. He lowered himself to the sloped earth beneath him, sitting cross-legged and patting the ground beside him. "Shhh. Look."

Essie sat gingerly, following the nod of his head. Together they watched the last slivers of light dance across the water's surface. A pair of velvet-antlered deer had stepped cautiously into the clearing on the far side, their eyes riveted on the questionable humans invading their space. When they saw there was no threat, they lowered their heads and ate, occasionally checking the status of their intruders.

Darkness came quickly, and along with it came a strange familiarity with this man beside her. Ryder had spoken of Shane years ago. Though she'd observed him this week, she still couldn't say she knew him. Yet she felt no sense of apprehension sitting alone with him in the cool night, listening to the water rush to its destination. His silence was sometimes disconcerting, but tonight was different. She sensed he wanted to linger...to talk.

"You have to overlook Ryder's manner, Essie. He's not what he seems." Shane turned toward her, and she could see the questions in his eyes. "And what about you, Essie Smith?"

She glanced down at the ground, then picked a purple wildflower near her feet. "What about me?" she asked, stalling for time.

"Why are you here, Essie? And don't tell me it's to cook."

As difficult as it was, she looked up at him. "I needed a job and a place to stay." At least this much was true and she could say it without blinking. "I lost my job at a warehouse and I thought it was time for a change."

"So you lied about your cooking experience." It wasn't a question, yet she answered him, anyway.

"Yes."

He smiled, seeming to respect her sudden candor. "I'd say your secret was safe with me, but it's not much of a secret—your not being a cook, I mean."

She straightened her back, feeling a little defensive. "But I'm learning. Hannah's a good teacher."

"Yes, she is." He studied her again in that mesmerizing way of his. "And yes, I'm sure you'll learn."

The sound of an engine in the distance made her turn. Ryder's pickup was throwing a trail of dust behind him as he tore down the road below. To Maddy's, no doubt. Why that hurt her so, she didn't know. It was crazy to still care about that man.

"I don't think Maddy's any competition."

She spun on him, throwing out words before she could think. "Who cares if she is?"

Shane held her glare and didn't respond for the longest time. When he finally spoke, his tone was less friendly. "I like you better when you speak the truth." He stood and untied his horse. "If you're ready to head back, I'll go with you."

Essie stayed seated and weighed her next words carefully. "My feelings for Ryder are confused right now."

Holding on to the reins, he stepped closer and looked down at her, his features relaxing. "That's better."

Impulsively, she asked what was really on her mind. "Why does he act so angry...so distant from the rest of you?"

"He's been away for years...rarely visited the ranch. When he did, he was always the same."

"But why?"

Shane hunkered down next to her, staring at the ground between them. "Our mother's death hit him the hardest."

Essie nodded her head. "Yes, I know."

His head turned slowly in her direction. He was studying her again, looking for the meaning behind her simple statement.

"I mean...well, Hannah told me about y-your mother." She knew she'd blown it again, but she kept trying. "Well...it's obvious. You and Josh seem so much more at ease with yourselves."

Shane's stare was unwavering. He knew there was more, and he was waiting for her to finish. But she couldn't. Someday she'd tell him the rest. But not yet.

His disappointment was obvious as he finally turned away and mounted his horse. Essie stepped into her own stirrup, flung her leg over the saddle and avoided Shane's eyes.

As she suspected that first day, this one was a hard man to fool.

* * *

Ryder spotted Maddy on the wicker porch swing looking wistfully over her lighted flower beds, and his heart went out to her as it always did these days. By the dim light, Billy played with a toy truck on a mound of dirt in the shadowy front yard. When he spotted Ryder he abandoned his toy and raced to the opening door of the pickup.

Ryder stooped and returned his quick hug. "How's it going, partner?"

"Do you have time to play trucks? Or maybe show me more rope tricks?" His blue eyes grew rounder with hope and excitement.

"Maybe later." Ryder tousled the boy's sandy hair and eyed the swing. "I need to talk with your mama for a while first. Okay, buddy?"

Billy looked disappointed, but didn't object. "Okay."

Ryder nudged him back to his truck, where a moment later he was making his usual "vroom-vroom" sound effects.

Ryder climbed the steps and sat next to Maddy. She reached over and rested a hand on his knee, and he covered it with a gentle squeeze.

"So how's it going, fair lady?" He did his best to put a smile in his voice, but it was growing more difficult with each visit.

Maddy offered her usual reassuring smile, one that no longer fooled either of them. "About the same." They swung back and forth in companionable silence for a while, watching Billy play. Eventually she handed him the big manila envelope that had been sitting on the lap of her pink satin robe. "My lawyer dropped this off earlier. I've read it over and signed it while he was here, and the girls witnessed it. This is your copy."

He stared at it, but didn't open it. He knew what it said. They'd been through it all before. Maybe later, when he was alone, he would read it over. But not now. Not in front of Billy. Matters of the heart, reduced to legalese. It still didn't sit right with him. He dropped the envelope onto the porch beside him and purposely chose another topic.

"You haven't changed your mind about coming to the ranch Saturday, now have you?"

She let out a small laugh. "I wouldn't miss it for the world, sugar." She shook her head, sending the ends of her long blond wig swinging from side to side. "Gee, I haven't laid eyes on Maxwell for years. Does he know I'm coming?"

Ryder chuckled, remembering the expression on his father's face when he'd heard. "Yep. They all know you're coming, Maddy." He turned his head and eyed her suspiciously. "You sure Josh and Shane have never met you?"

She looked straight ahead. "No, sir. Never had the pleasure."

Whether she was telling the truth or protecting the guilty, Ryder knew he'd never learn from Maddy. Her morals might be questionable to many, but as madam of the Purple Palace, she did have her own code of ethics. And one was never to name clients. If, as a kid, Ryder hadn't seen for himself his father leave this house, he never would have known he'd been here. He thought again about asking Maddy if she'd been the one his father had come to visit, but he knew she'd never say. Besides, he wasn't sure he wanted to know.

She stood and walked slowly to the railing, leaning on it before she spoke. "Billy...time to wash up for bed."

"Ah, Mom—"

"Come on, now. Do as I say."

"But Ryder said—"

Ryder walked to Maddy's side. "How about a story in bed tonight, instead?"

Billy angled his dirt-smudged face. "Not from a book? One of your own?"

Ryder looked at his watch. "If you're in bed in ten minutes."

Billy tore up the steps and slammed the screen door behind him.

Maddy looked after him, then eyed Ryder, a glassy sheen

covering her heavy-lidded eyes. "He adores you, sugar. I'm so grateful for that."

Ryder couldn't look at her another moment. He pulled her into a light embrace, working his palm in a circle between her shoulder blades. "Me, too, Maddy. Me, too." They stood that way till a car pulled into the side entrance.

The front door was reserved for Maddy, Billy and friends who came for social visits with the pair. Customers knew to use the side door. With the wide wraparound porch, it was difficult to discern which was the main entrance, but the ladies who worked and lived there knew, and so did their clientele.

Ryder glanced at his watch. "Think I'll go in and see if Billy's ready." Maddy walked with him toward the back of the house and the only two bedrooms on the first floor. Billy saw them coming and jumped between his jungle print sheets.

"Did you brush your teeth?" Maddy asked, leaning over to kiss his forehead. Instead of answering, he clicked his bottom and top rows of teeth together and offered a shining display, evidence of a new tooth barely breaking the gum line over the gap.

She brushed hair off his forehead and smiled down at him. "Very good. Night, sweetheart. Sleep tight."

"Don't let the bed bugs bite," Billy said, snuggling lower under his covers. Maddy let herself out, blowing Billy one last kiss before shutting the door.

Ryder sat wearily on the edge of the bed, tugged off his boots, then settled alongside the squiggly youngster, who fit easily under the crook of his arm.

"Okay. Which one do you want to hear?"

"The one about you and that mean ol' grizzly bear."

With one arm bent beneath his head, he used the other to pull Billy closer. "It was late November and the snow was knee-deep...."

Maddy leaned against the wall and listened from the other side of the door. She closed her eyes and expelled a long sigh. "Thank you, Lord, for this gift. I know I probably don't deserve any of your favors. But it's mighty nice that you're seeing to my Billy.''

Slowly she walked past the connecting bathroom to her own bedroom, swallowing the tears she refused to shed.

Five

Essie put away the last clean dish and untied her apron. Hannah had already retired to her room to watch television, and Essie was feeling restless. A good book and a good night's sleep would have been the practical thing to do. She'd barely slept the three nights since arriving, and she was exhausted. Last night was the worst. Images of Ryder leaning closer, his lips so close to hers, had kept her tossing and turning for hours.

She trudged up the back stairs to her room and splashed cold water on her face, hoping to revive herself. The bottle of Hawaiian Breezes perfume sat on the countertop. Quickly she hid it behind some towels in the cabinet below. She'd worn no other fragrance since high school. It seemed strange not using it today, but she wouldn't take another chance of sparking Ryder's memory. Not till she was ready to tell him the truth of who she was would she wear it again.

A cool breeze blew the white Priscilla curtains away from the window near her bed. She walked over and closed it, spotting the object of her dreams as he disappeared into the stables. She hesitated only a second, then grabbed a sweater from the corner rocker and darted down the stairs.

As she crossed the gravel drive, a strong headwind slowed her progress. The temperature had dropped at least thirty degrees, and now she wished she'd worn something warmer. She pushed on toward the stables, anxiety making her shake as much as the cold. She had no plan in going to him, just to be with him. Sometimes, like tonight, he felt like a magnet she couldn't resist, though logic told her she probably should. But for nearly half of her lifetime, logic had little to do with her feelings for Ryder Malone.

He was putting fresh hay in the stall with the bay and her new foal as she rubbed the sleeves of her sweater and walked toward him. When he finished his task, he wiped his hands on his jeans and saw her. She averted her gaze and looked at the foal instead, stopping to lean on the gate.

"He's not quite so shaky today," she said as the foal stepped behind his mother.

"Yes...but you are," Ryder said. He wrapped an arm around her shoulders, sliding his hand up and down her sleeve.

Even through the sweater, she felt the heat of his touch, which did nothing to still her shakes. It was as if the clock had been turned back fifteen years to the day she met him. She still felt like an adolescent with blemishes, braces and an extra fifty pounds. Why was it that whenever she was with him, her confidence seemed nonexistent?

Still shaking, he turned her toward him and started buttoning the sweater she'd hastily pulled around her. He started with the top button and worked his way down slowly, methodically, his eyes focused on each round piece. He talked to the buttons instead of her face.

"I'm surprised you own something that starts at your chin."

She watched his lips form a teasing smile, but then her gaze followed his fingers. They were at her waist and there were four more buttons. She could feel her blood pooling lower in her jeans, racing to keep up with his hands, making her legs feel as unsteady as the young foal's.

When he'd finished the last button, his gaze traveled up and met hers. All she could do was search his handsome face, the dark brown hair that skimmed the collar of his denim jacket, the troubled brown eyes that showed more sadness than anger tonight. His hands trailed up and down her arms, trying to warm her, which made her tremble more. She remembered the promise she'd made to herself only yesterday and stepped in closer, resting her hands on either side of his hips, tilting her face up to him. She'd make it as easy as possible for him, but if he didn't take the bait, she'd take the initiative.

She fixed her gaze on his lips. They weren't moving closer, but they weren't backing away, either. She closed the small space between them, feeling his rock-hard thighs now against hers. Her hands moved to his back, stroking it lightly.

Then his lips began the long journey to hers, one that seemed as though it were in slow motion. Instead of meeting them, she stared as they came closer, not believing the moment had finally arrived. She licked her lips, hoping he would like what he felt, already knowing she would. His hands gripped her shoulders tighter and then he lifted his chin. He kissed her gently on the forehead and backed away.

She didn't know which to do—kick him in the shins or scream. Instead, she freed her hands from behind him and clamped them on both sides of his head. With one last hot glare, she pulled his lips to hers and took what she wanted. She felt him stiffen briefly, but she persisted, parting his lips with her tongue. When he wrapped his arms around her back and returned her kiss, she moaned into his mouth, her arms winding tighter around his neck. His tongue roved the dark recesses of her mouth, seeking, giving. She returned his ardor with more of her own. He lifted her off her feet, sliding her along the firmness that bulged beneath his belt. She groaned again, tilting her head for a deeper kiss. She was no longer cold, but still she trembled with the need for more.

Suddenly he set her away from him, stiff-arming her, his fingers biting into her shoulders. He shook his head back and forth, and she could see his chest heaving much like her own. Till his breathing slowed, he stared at the ground between them. Eventually he raised his head.

"Essie...you don't want to get mixed up with the likes of me—"

"Yes, I do." She interrupted, the truth of her words overriding pride.

"I...I can't do this." He turned to the gate and rested both elbows against the top. His head hung between his hunched shoulders as he stared at nothing. "There's so much you don't know—"

"Then tell me," she persisted. She knew more than he thought, but she sensed something specific weighed on his mind tonight.

He pivoted back to her and started to speak, then closed his mouth and turned away. Before she could think of the right words to say, he pushed off the gate and walked toward his horse, which she hadn't noticed till now was saddled and ready to ride. He pulled the brown quarter horse out, mounted him and looked back at her with eyes that were once again shielded.

"I'm sorry. I have to go." He held her gaze an agonizing moment, then left without another word.

She stepped clear of the stables and watched him push his horse to a gallop. He was headed down the same trail he'd taken last night. The one that led to Maddy's.

Essie saddled her sorrel as quickly as she could and a moment later was on his trail. What she hoped to accomplish, she didn't know. But one thing was certain: she had to see where this Maddy lived. Maybe if the woman greeted him at the door with a kiss like the one she'd just had, then maybe, just maybe, she would believe Ryder truly cared about this woman. Till then, she couldn't, she wouldn't. Something wasn't right. He couldn't have responded to her the way he had if he felt deeply about someone else. Years may have changed him some, but not that much.

The farther down the trail she rode, the more she worried what she might discover. And if they had gone inside, what would she do then? She raced along, her mind working as hard as the horse. Then the idea came to her. Earlier Max had suggested cocktails at six and dinner at seven or seven-thirty. He'd said to ask Ryder if that would be too late for Billy. She certainly didn't have to get her answer now at Maddy's, but it was the only excuse she could come up with. She'd started this chase and, by golly, she would finish.

After twenty minutes in the saddle, she wondered if she was on the right trail. Ryder was nowhere in sight. But when she followed the next curve, she found herself in a clearing. At the bottom of a gentle slope she saw a single home, a huge old Victorian painted purple with white and pink trim. She stopped and took it in. The shape of the home, with its wide curving porch and turrets that rose three floors, was breathtaking, but the colors were so garish. Her first thought was what a waste of a beautiful home. Why would anyone choose such colors? Then she spotted Ryder's horse tied to a hitching post and all thoughts of style were forgotten.

She swore under her breath, realizing he must have gone inside already. Then she noticed a Lincoln Town Car and a pickup, too, making the whole motley scene seem surreal. And suddenly, going to the door seemed the boldest thing she'd ever done. Surely she would make a fool of herself. Tomorrow was only Thursday. She could tell Ryder later about the times for Saturday and he could call and ask Maddy. This had to be the lamest excuse for walking up to the woman's door she could think of.

Yet that's exactly what she did.

She tied her horse and walked up the steps, debating a moment which door to use. She decided on the one closest to the parked cars. With her hand shaking, she lifted it and knocked softly on the wood next to the ornate leaded glass.

Footsteps approached and she nearly bolted. She took a deep breath and exhaled as the door swung inward.

"Why, come on in, sweetie. Now, who might you be?"

Essie stood riveted to the porch and tried not to stare, but the woman wore more makeup than Tammy Faye Bakker, and she had on the frilliest hot pink negligee Essie had ever seen. Eventually she shut her mouth and thrust out her hand.

"My name is Essie." This couldn't be Maddy, could it? She had to be forty-five, if she was a day, but that was the least of it.

"Essie…Essie?" The woman cocked her head, batted her long fake eyelashes and tapped a dangerous looking fingernail to her chin. "Hmm…can't say as I ever heard of anyone called Essie." Now she blatantly sized up the newcomer from head to toe. "Well, come on in, Essie. Let's have a look at you."

Why she crossed that threshold, Essie would never know, but she did, instantly taking in the heavily draped parlor— purple velvet divans, fringed floor lamps, gaudy pieces of sculpture and more gilding than the set of Sunset Boulevard. While she was gaping, the woman reached out for Essie and began unbuttoning her sweater.

Essie slapped her hand away. "What are you doing?"

"Now don't be shy." A younger woman sashayed into the parlor, her gaze also assessing. "We just need to see what you're hiding under there."

The room was warm and she didn't need the sweater. But she wasn't about to be undressed by these strange women. Essie began unbuttoning her own sweater, returning the new woman's stare. Unlike the older one, she wore a bustiette and a short spandex skirt, both in black. She looked to be in her thirties, but still not Maddy material. *Please, not Maddy.*

"May I ask what your names are?" Essie asked, reaching the bottom button.

The one in pink said, "Call me Suzette." She extended

her arm in the direction of the younger woman who wiggled over. "And this is Madonna."

Figured.

"Rachel should be down in a bit."

Essie forced a smile, which brought Suzette charging forward. In one graceful sweep, she removed the bulky sweater and then gasped.

"My, my." She turned to her partner. "Lookie what we have here? Tiny waist and big knockers!"

Essie grabbed her sweater back and held it in front of her, feeling her cheeks turn crimson. Of all the nerve. What kind of women were these? She heard a giggle coming from the spiral staircase to the left and looked up. A cowboy with a dung-eating grin was draped all over a giggling young woman in red underwear, complete with red garters, black stockings and four-inch red spiked heels.

Oh...my...God. Essie knew her mouth was open wide enough to catch flies, but she couldn't help it. She thought these houses existed only in movies. And here she was, looking as if she were...were what? Did they think she was applying for a job? She turned back to the woman in pink with the Dolly Parton wig.

"Here comes Rachel now."

"Excuse me. I think there's been a mistake—" As she turned to leave, she looked out the side window. And there he was.

Ryder was standing next to a beautiful woman dressed modestly in a long gray sweater and matching pants. She had long, straight blond hair and was very thin, and from this distance she appeared to be at least fifteen years Ryder's senior. But what drew Essie's eye was the little towheaded boy with a missing front tooth who stood alongside. Ryder was gazing down at the boy with an expression she had never seen, and her stomach knotted. In the next instant, Ryder picked the boy up, and his chubby little arms circled Ryder's neck, his legs locking behind Ryder's waist. Essie heard the women talking to her and wanted to look away from the tender scene in the garden, but she couldn't. It was as if time had stopped...and her heart along with it.

Finally she forced herself to face the women. "I—I'm sorry. I must have the wrong house." Over their protests, she turned and ran for her horse, hoping Ryder wouldn't spot her before she could escape.

She pushed the horse as fast as she dared till she reached the top of the path and found refuge behind the trees. Then she pulled on the reins and slowed her pace, her heart in her throat and her chest convulsing.

What a fool she'd been. To have thought coming to Montana might solve the puzzle of Ryder Malone! And following him to that house tonight like some love-starved puppy! Though seeing him back there with Billy proved he was the man she'd fallen in love with in Detroit, it only made matters worse. She'd seen his tough-guy mask slip before, when they were kids. But seeing him with Maddy and her child...probably his child...proved something she'd dreaded from the inception of this foolhardy plan. She'd waited too long to find him. There was someone else in his life now.

She was too late.

"Are you sure about this, sugar? It's not too late to change your mind?"

Ryder gave Billy a last hug and set him down, keeping an arm around the boy's narrow shoulders. "I'm positive. I'll be back tomorrow and Friday, too, when I'm done with work. Then Saturday night we'll all go to the ranch."

Maddy touched Ryder's arm and he smiled as he waved goodbye to Billy and walked away. He passed the visiting Lincoln and pickup and mounted his horse. There was no turning back now, he thought, pushing his horse into an easy lope. It was the right thing to do. He rode along the ridge, his heart heavy with the days and weeks ahead. He wished he could feel good about his decision. But *good* just didn't fit.

He took his time weaving his way through the tangled

thicket that had overgrown the trail to the ranch. Over the tops of cottonwood trees he could see the MoJoes and the retreating sunlight. At one high point he spotted the ranch and the lower meadows where the cattle had spent the winter.

The constant gurgle and whoosh of the stream lulled him along, making him wish he could ride on forever. Where or when, he didn't care, so he let his horse take him where it would. A strange noise perked its ears and its head came around toward the stream. Ryder stopped and listened. At first he thought it was an animal in distress, and he pointed his horse down toward it. Then he saw the lone figure, her back to a fallen aspen, her face buried in her hands. Her horse nickered softly as they approached.

Ryder scanned the area for signs of a fall or struggle, but the ground seemed undisturbed. Only Essie seemed out of sorts. He thought about turning around before she saw him, letting her unleash her sadness in private. Yet the sound of her anguish couldn't be ignored. It came from somewhere so deep, so real, that it felt like a place Ryder knew too well.

He heaved a sigh and nudged his horse ahead, letting it stop to drink its own reflection from the stream about a dozen yards beyond. The last thing he needed was another woman's problem, he thought, as he dismounted and wrapped the reins around a shrub.

When she heard him approach she turned her back to him. He could see her wiping her face on the sleeves of her sweater and heard her sniffle when he sat cross-legged on a patch of moss beside her.

When she didn't speak, he asked, "Would you rather I leave you alone?"

She sniffed again and turned slowly, her eyes on the stream in front of them. There was something oddly familiar in her profile and, again, the notion that they may have met before crossed his mind. He studied her, trying to remember something, but nothing rang a bell. Except the memory of his mother crying. And much later Maddy. It seemed his destiny to be surrounded by unhappy women. He fished a clean handkerchief from his hip pocket and gave it to Essie.

She wiped her eyes and nose, then glanced at him for only a second before the flood returned. He watched and waited, feeling like an intruder, yet unable to walk away. Whatever it was, it hurt bad. And hurting was something he understood.

Finally she used the handkerchief again and spoke softly between gulps of air. "I...I made such a fool of myself...back at the stables earlier...and now a-at that—" she waved at the purple house "—that house."

"You were there?"

"Yes. Please don't ask me why I went—"

"Essie, Essie. Shhh." He shook his head and stroked her soft, brown hair. "I don't know what you saw back there, but it's not what you think—"

With more spunk in her voice, she frowned and asked, "You mean it's not a house of ill repute?"

Ryder laughed. "Haven't heard it called *that* in a while." He sobered quickly when he saw she found no humor in the situation. "Yes, it's one of those houses...but I wasn't there because—"

"I saw you in the yard with Billy. That was Billy, wasn't it?"

He looked away. "Yes."

"And Maddy?"

His gaze came back to hers. "Yes, that was Maddy, but—"

She held up a hand. "I'm sorry. You don't owe me any explanation."

"Essie—" He looked down at her, feeling more than he understood, more than he knew was wise at this time in his life. "I didn't go there to be with Maddy...not in the way you think. It's Billy." He saw the confusion in her tear-streaked face. "What I mean is...Billy needs me. I've been going there as often as possible to play with him." He picked up a stone and skipped it across the water. "As you can imagine, the men who frequent that place couldn't care less about any madam's kid.''

"M-Maddy is the madam?"

"She never refers to herself as that, but yes, she is. Her mother owned the Purple Palace before she died. Now Maddy runs it. She hasn't had…you know, clients…in a long time." He knew he sounded defensive, but it was true. Maddy was a good woman, doing the best she could under difficult circumstances.

Essie looked at him with blue eyes so sad…and so familiar. She seemed to be searching his face for something. The truth, maybe. But what truth? And there was turmoil etched on her forehead, as if she were debating whether to tell him the source of her pain. A part of him wanted to ask her what it was, yet he remained silent, knowing too well the need to keep one's own counsel.

Her lips started to quiver, then she spoke, her voice so low he could barely hear her. "Do you have a bedroll on your horse?" She hugged herself, and he saw that she was shaking.

He nodded slowly, then went to his horse and returned, untying the bedroll and draping it around her back.

"Thank you," she said, sounding as though the storm had passed. "C-can we just talk for a while? Do you have to go?"

With the pad of his thumb he erased a smudge below one of her eyes. "No, I don't have to go." Though staying felt risky. Nonetheless, he leaned back on his elbows and eyed her, wondering what was on her mind, what had upset her so.

"D-do you mind if I ask where you've been all these years?" He frowned, not certain what she meant, then she added, "I mean…well, I heard you'd been away from the ranch for a long time. I—I was just curious where you lived—"

"Oh. Helena. Worked a big ranch there…from the time I graduated till a month ago." They regarded each other for a while, and he wondered where this was leading. Cer-

tainly his whereabouts had nothing to do with her tears.
That he should care what had caused them, concerned him.

"Why did you come back?"

He'd expected her to ask why he had left and was relieved when she hadn't. "Ah, that's an easy one. Billy. I
wanted to have a hand in raising him." He saw the pain
on her face before she looked away. Did she think the boy
was his? And if she did, what of it? The conversation
stalled and he thought she was finished, then she turned
back.

"Didn't you miss your brothers?"

He thought for a moment before answering. It wasn't an
easy question. "Sometimes." He wasn't sure this was a
topic he wanted to explore. "We got split up when we were
young…each went to different schools for a while, then
college. Distance has a way of making even loved ones
seem like strangers." Her chin quivered and he thought she
might cry again. She didn't, but she stopped talking and
started to shiver. Without thinking, he sat up and reached
around her, wrapping the bedroll tighter, his face close to
hers as he did. Too close. So close that he knew he was in
trouble. He could see the tears spiking on her lower lashes.

Finally she whispered, "Would you kiss me again?"

He knew he *shouldn't*. And he knew he *wanted* to. He
also knew he'd never been good at managing matters of
the heart. Against all reason he wrapped his arms around
her trembling shoulders and pulled her damp face to his
chest, hoping to bring her some measure of comfort this
way, instead.

She slipped her hands beneath his jacket and circled his
waist as she had in the barn and, in that instant, he knew
should had lost to *want*. There was no way he would leave
her here alone, and she wasn't ready to move. But by staying, he would doom them both to regrets come tomorrow.

Yet the night had needs of its own.

Not just hers, but his.

Six

Essie pulled back and gazed into Ryder's dark eyes. Even in the moonlight, she could see the desire there, mixed with worry. Worry for what, she wasn't sure. That kissing her would somehow hurt her, lead her on? Or that he would be betraying another woman? His lips lowered to her forehead and brushed her cold skin. No, he wasn't betraying Maddy. He didn't love her. He'd as much as said it before, hadn't he? And now, with his hands rubbing her back so protectively...she was certain he cared about her. Essie or Savannah—it didn't matter at this moment. Only that he cared about the woman he held so tenderly. She knew, as she always had, that Ryder would never hurt her.

She tilted her face up, forcing his lips away from her forehead. His eyes met hers briefly, then lowered to her lips. She watched him coming closer, knowing she would have her kiss...and, at long last, so much more.

His lips met hers, warm and gentle, but quickly grew impatient, as impatient as her own. She couldn't find a deep enough spot. Her tongue probed and probed as did his, their groans coming husky and in unison. It was as if she wanted every inch of his body to enter hers, to become so totally one that she would lose sight of where he started and she ended.

She tugged his jacket from him and tore at the buttons of his flannel shirt, her mouth never leaving his. Just as greedily, he freed her from her sweater and slid both hands under the elastic of her bra, exposing her fully to his warm hands. Whether it was his moan or hers that echoed through the still night, she didn't know.

His lips left her mouth and claimed a nipple, licking her to full arousal, while his thumb worked the other. His tongue trailed up her neck and she laid back against the bedroll, taking him with her. He spread himself atop her, his rigid sex pressing against her inner thighs. Her blood rushed hot and fast to the area that waited impatiently to be explored, leaving her dizzy and breathless. She grappled with his zipper, tugging his jeans and briefs as low as she could reach. He sat up and finished the job for her, his eyes not leaving hers, his breath as ragged as her own. For years she had dreamed of this moment, of taking it slow, making it last for hours. But she knew it wouldn't be like that. She wanted him now. This very moment.

He slid her jeans free while she shed the rest of her clothes, tossing them aside. He lowered himself to her again and she felt every curve and plane of him pressed against her own naked flesh. She wrapped her feet behind his knees, holding him as close as she could, feeling the tip of his sex against the hot and wet space between her legs. She bit her top lip so hard she thought it might bleed, forcing herself not to shout out her wish.

Please. Now.

His breath was hot on her neck as he kissed her there and then her ear, the sound roaring louder than the beat of her heart. She turned her face into his mouth and claimed it again, more possessively than before. A growling noise came deep from her throat and into his mouth. She could feel his excitement pulsing against her most sensitive spot, more moisture preparing the way. Her ankles locked behind his waist holding him captive. She would leave no doubt in his mind what she wanted.

She vaguely felt his hand leave her breast and trail down her side to the place where all her feeling centered. When his finger entered her, she cried aloud. Even this was more than she'd imagined. His touch so inflamed her she wanted to roll him over and impale herself on him. Never had she felt so greedy, so impatient. Suddenly it felt as though she would never get enough of him. If this night never ended, it wouldn't be enough.

Her breasts pushed against his heaving chest with each gulp for air. She lifted her hips to him and he directed himself into her ever so slowly, barely breaking the plane, the soft skin of his head rubbing back and forth across her swollen flesh. The smell of sage had been replaced with the hot scent of his naked flesh and the moisture they created between them. She opened her eyes and saw nothing but the endless starry sky over his broad shoulder. Then suddenly there were streaks of light shooting behind her eyelids as she pressed them tightly closed. She felt hot liquid rush from her and puddle beneath her. Still he only entered her by measured degrees. She knew there would be pain, but she couldn't wait another moment. Pressing her hands against his cool backside she pushed him to the wall—the wall she'd always known he would be the one to break.

Unexpectedly, he pulled out of her and stared into her eyes, shock registering on his handsome face. "Essie—?"

She could feel the tears streaking down her temples. "Please, Ryder. Please..."

He lowered himself to her again, taking her in his arms and holding her tight. "You sure?"

She turned her lips to his ear and spoke her heart. "I've never been more sure." She kissed his neck till he turned his lips to hers and kissed her gently, with quick, light kisses, as though he treasured her and held her more dear.

Slowly, carefully, he entered her again, till finally he was inside her fully. The pain was replaced with such a fullness, she marveled at the fit of them, knowing for certain she had waited for the right man, the only one who could complete her so.

He started moving inside her and she matched his rhythm, meeting each thrust with one of her own. Her flesh felt swollen and sore, but she didn't want him to stop, to leave that space she had saved for him that would never feel complete till he put himself between her legs again.

Somewhere in the recesses of her mind, she wondered if there would be an again. But there had to be. Nothing could feel so perfect, so right. He had to feel it, too. There would be a lifetime of tonights.

His thrusts came harder and faster, and she struggled to keep up with him, her lungs devoid of air. Till finally she felt his body quiver above her and she felt a sudden thick heat rush from him to her. Gently he placed his weight to one side of her, still covering her with half of him, his breath hot against her neck as he nibbled little kisses there.

He reached across her and pulled part of the bedroll over her, keeping her warm. Locked together, she rolled into him, covering him, too, from the cold night air. She heard an owl in the distance and the stream beside them, sounds that had escaped her while she'd lived through the fantasy she'd imagined for so long.

His arms tightened around her, and she snuggled closer, her fingers trailing over the wet hairs of his chest. It hadn't been a mistake, after all—coming to Montana, finding him again. In the comfort of his arms, she wondered if now was the time to tell him who she was. Would it spoil things if he knew she'd deceived him? Or would he understand and forgive her? Maybe he'd make love to her again…here in the moonlight.

His breathing slowed and he rolled onto his back, breaking their union. He kept one arm under her neck and bent the other beneath his head. The silence she'd enjoyed just moments ago suddenly felt oppressive. Something weighed on his mind. She could feel it, and it scared her. When the time came for him to speak, she knew it wouldn't be words of love. Physically he remained close, but mentally she knew he'd already left.

Essie lay very still, afraid to move, knowing the fantasy was about to end. In its wake would follow something far less than she was prepared for.

"Essie…"

Just the way he said her name foreshadowed her fears.

"You should have told me. I never would have—"

"But I wanted you to." She inched closer, showing him she had no regrets.

"It was selfish of me. I'm sorry—"

"Shhh." She wrapped her arm around his waist. "Please don't spoil it."

He sat up, breaking contact. The cold night air rushed over her, accompanied by the dread of what might come next.

"I…I can't get involved with anyone right now." He stared at the stream beside them as if she were no longer there.

The word *why* stuck in her throat, refusing to voice itself. If he didn't want to be with her, what was the difference why? Could it hurt less to know? She doubted it. Though, by the ache in her chest, she also doubted it could hurt worse.

Oh, Ryder, Ryder. She reached out for his back, but stopped short. No matter how she felt, she wouldn't beg. For all intents and purposes, she'd practically begged for what she'd already got. Nothing short of his love would ever work.

But why? The word still wanted out.

She watched him dressing, shards of moonbeam filtering through the cottonwoods. He didn't look at her. Instead, he acted as if he couldn't wait to be as far away as possible.

Essie sat up, clutching the bedroll to her chest, wishing he would hurry and leave. The sob at the back of her throat pushed and wouldn't go down. She wouldn't let him see her cry again. Look what had happened before. He'd pitied her, only tried to comfort her, and she'd all but made it impossible for him to say no. With such a blatant invitation, what man would have?

He stood at her side, fully clothed. "I can't leave you here alone."

She tried to talk, but couldn't. She bit her top lip to keep the tears at bay.

"Come on, Essie. I'll ride with you back to the ranch."

She could see by his stance he wasn't going anywhere. With great effort she forced out her words. "I'd rather be by myself." More than anything she longed for the privacy of her own bed.

He looked away as he spoke. "If you insist. Why don't you get dressed, and I'll watch you ride from here...make sure you make it back safely."

She staggered to her feet, taking the bedroll with her. He kept his back to her while she dressed, which she did as quickly as she could. Strange, she thought, walking to her horse, she'd felt so natural naked with this man. Now they couldn't even look at each other fully clothed.

She mounted her sorrel, feeling her bruised flesh against the saddle. She let her horse set its own pace as she left, self-pity keeping her company as it ambled off. She wondered if this was how Eve felt when she left the Garden of Eden, after she'd talked Adam into taking that bite of apple. Except she didn't know what her sin had been back there at the stream. How could something that had seemed so magical, so right, have been so wrong?

She was still asking herself that same question when she left the stable and headed for the house. In the distance she could see the silhouette of Ryder on his horse as he turned slowly and rode back the way he came. Back to Maddy and his son, no doubt.

She trudged up the back stairs, each step reminding her of his entry into her body. For sure she didn't mourn the loss of her virginity. And it was too easy to say she simply mourned the loss of Ryder.

At last she stood in the shower and let the tears flow.

Yes, she would miss Ryder. But more, she'd miss the small degree of confidence she'd only just begun to feel. She lathered herself and hunched beneath the hot spray. Once again, she felt like the homely little fat girl she'd been for most of her life.

For the better part of the night, Essie rehearsed how she would act when she saw Ryder at breakfast. Now it was time to put her resolve into action.

At five-thirty she walked down the stairs and saw Hannah bent over the sink. As difficult as it might be, Essie reminded herself to act as though it were any other morning. No one need know…unless Ryder told them, which seemed unlikely. If he were the kiss-and-tell sort, surely he would have told her something about Maddy or the others from the Purple Palace when the subject came up last night. Instead he had seemed tight-lipped.

When she carried her first tray into the dining room, she expelled a nervous breath and stopped just inside the swinging door. Joshua was talking to Shane about irrigation ditches for the new crop of hay. Max was reading his paper and ignoring the pair.

Ryder's chair was empty.

Maybe she should feel relieved, but she didn't. She wanted their first "morning after" behind her. Now she would have to deal with the anticipation and knot in her stomach for who knew how long. Would he show for lunch? Supper?

She set bowls in the center of the table and felt the ache of her back teeth from grinding them too hard. Damn him for prolonging the inevitable.

"Speaking of the ditches—" Shane drank some coffee "—I passed Ryder in the stable. He said he fixed your Cat last night. He's probably out there using it now…getting a head start."

Essie took her time at the side table with her back to the men.

"He fixed it last night?" Joshua sounded surprised.

"Hmm. I'd have thought he'd be at the Purple Palace instead of the equipment barn." He laughed and so did Shane and Max.

Essie turned as Josh shook his head and spoke again.

"Huh! That guy never ceases to surprise me. Just when you think you have him figured out—"

Essie pushed at the kitchen door and stomped to the counter to make more toast. Just when you think you have him figured out... Oh, Josh. You don't know the half of it.

Lunch and supper were just as frustrating as breakfast. Ryder was nowhere in sight. Essie thought about taking a walk, but the thought of running into him alone seemed worse. So after the dishes were done, she helped herself to a large bowl of homemade ice cream and went to her room. Behind the closed door, she puffed out her cheeks and let loose a long, loud sigh. At least here, in the sanctuary of her room, she didn't have to pretend. She didn't have to smile and ignore this feeling that her heart had been torn from her chest.

She dropped into her rocker by the window, but refused to look out, concentrating instead on the chunks of strawberries, nuts and real whipped cream on top of the ice cream. It was her second bowl today. Before that there were brownies and Hannah's hot pastries. She unfastened her jeans and pulled her legs up under her.

Old habits died hard. For years she'd resisted the urge to overeat when things went wrong. Even when relationships ended and later when she lost her job at the warehouse, she'd stuck to a healthy diet.

But desperate situations called for desperate measures. And eating would most likely be her only physical pleasure for some time. A flash of Ryder hovering over her by the stream streaked across her mind, a pleasure so intense she knew it would never come again. Quickly she shoved another spoonful in her mouth and blocked out the memory.

After the dessert came the guilt followed by the sense of despair. Finally at nine o'clock she picked up the phone on her nightstand and dialed Jenny's number.

"Hello?" A sleepy voice answered after the fifth ring.

"It's me. Did I wake you up?" She'd forgotten about the difference in time.

"That's okay." She yawned into the receiver, then sounded like the old Jenny. "I had to get up to answer the phone, anyway." She chuckled, then in the next breath sounded somber. "Savannah? What's wrong?"

"Does something have to be wrong for me to call you?" Before the glib answer got out, there was a catch at the back of her throat and she knew tears were close behind.

"Savannahhh—?"

"God, I wish you were here. I could use a hug." She sniffed once but held on.

There was silence on the other end of the phone, and for a moment Essie thought she'd lost the connection. Then Jenny spoke again.

"Would day after tomorrow be soon enough?"

"What are you talking about? I'm not ready to throw in the towel yet." Why, she wasn't sure. What did she hope to accomplish by staying?

"Maybe not. But I'm ready for a vacation. Unless you don't want me to come—"

"Are you kidding?" Essie sprang from the rocker, her jeans falling to her knees. She laughed aloud, surprised she had it in her. "But can you get away this time of year?"

"We got a new batch of college kids cooking up a storm. And I've been working a lot of overtime, freezing as much as storage will hold." Her voice turned down a bit. "It's been so quiet here at the apartment, I've been working later and later."

"But the airline ticket—"

"Not to worry, girlfriend. I've been stashing money away left and right. Besides, one of the bosses mentioned a frequent-flyer ticket he couldn't use that was about to expire. I'll ask him about it first thing tomorrow."

"How long can you stay?"

"One or two weeks. Depends."

"On what?"

"How long you can put up with me."

"Make it two. I might need your help moving." As soon as the words were out, she realized her mistake. She hadn't told Jenny she would be staying in Montana, even though she was more certain than ever she couldn't stay at the ranch for long.

"I was right, wasn't I?" There was no happiness in her voice now. "You're staying out there."

"Yes."

"But not at the ranch?"

"It's a long story, Jen. I'd rather talk about it face-to-face on Saturday. Yikes!"

"What is it?"

"Saturday. I forgot. There's a big dinner party here for Ryder's birthday."

"Then I'll come Sunday instead."

"Nonsense. Just a sec. Let me think." She pulled up her jeans and paced back and forth as far as the phone cord could reach. Then it came to her. "Call me back when you know your flight time. I'll have Shane or Josh—whoever's available—pick you up. I wish I could, Jen, but there's a lot of cooking and it would take at least three hours if I go."

"Shane or Josh, huh? How old did you say these brothers were?" The old mischief was back in her voice, and Essie laughed.

"Josh is only twenty-five. Hmm. Shane's thirty-two, though, just a little older than you. Think I'll ask him first."

"I don't know. Young stuff is in these days."

Essie smiled into the receiver. "Gee, it good to hear your voice." Essie swallowed hard. She'd made it this far, she wouldn't cave in now.

"Is there anything I can bring?"

"Yes!" She practically shouted. "Some of my clothes, you bum. The nights get colder than you think out here. A few flannel shirts would help."

"Yeah, but I bet you got some mileage out of my sexier stuff."

Yes, she did. And she knew Jenny would worm the whole story out of her eventually. Though she didn't want to broach the subject now, she needed Jenny's help with another item. She could buy it herself the next trip to town, but she didn't know if she'd be alone.

She exhaled into the phone. "I'd like you to bring something else—" She hesitated, then let the words come out in a rush. "Please don't ask me now—I promise we'll talk when you get here—but could you bring me one of those test kits?"

A couple of beats passed and Jenny stuttered. "I—I'm afraid to ask, but what kind of test kit are we talking about here?"

"The kind that sometimes turns blue after a few minutes." She held her breath and waited for the barrage of questions, but none came.

"Will do. Anything else?"

The few tears that clung to her lower lashes finally fell. "I love you, Jenny Moon."

"I'll call you back with the flight times. Hang in there, kiddo. Love and hugs are on the way."

Essie hung up the phone and danced across the room. Jenny was coming to Montana. For two weeks. She dropped on the side of the bed, feeling better than she thought she would ever feel again. She flopped back spread-eagle and stared at the oscillating fan overhead.

What if Jenny liked Montana and decided to stay? They could find a place together. She could find something more suited to her skills, and Jenny could cook anywhere, maybe even here. She sat up quickly, her mind racing.

All was not lost yet.

Seven

Unlike yesterday, Essie flew down the stairs to the kitchen, humming a nameless tune. The situation with Ryder two days ago still occupied space, but she restricted it to the backlands of her mind, eager for the moment Jenny would walk through the door.

Hannah was pulling food from the refrigerator and setting things on the counter. "Crowd's light this mornin'. Josh flew in and outta here a minute ago. Took a Thermos a coffee and a bag a muffins. Near as I can tell, Ryder didn't come home last night so doubt he'll be here, either."

Good, Essie thought, starting on some French toast batter. Let him hide out. Tonight he would have to show his face for the birthday party and that would be soon enough. Besides, she and Jenny could escape upstairs as soon as the dishes were done. One way or the other, she wouldn't let that man keep her down.

Shane came in the back door and helped himself to a mug of coffee and nodded his hello as he started to pass through.

"Shane?" Her request would be a terrible imposition, but there seemed little choice. He stopped with his back to the connecting swinging door. "I could use a big favor from you today."

He eyed her over his steaming mug, took a sip and waited. A man of few words. Poor Jen. What a long ride home she'll have! "My best friend is coming to visit." His gaze narrowed as if to say What has this to do with me? "She's flying in later this morning."

"And I can't spare her a second t'day," Hannah piped in. "So you'll be a nice young man and pick her up, won'tcha?"

Without so much as a grimace, he asked, "What time?"

"Eleven-thirty...in Billings. I've written the flight number and her name on the back of her picture." Essie dug in her hip pocket and found the photo. Shane came over and took it from her. He stared at the pictured woman, who had a tanned and pretty face, big brown eyes and hair similar to Essie's, only darker like his own.

"Eleven-thirty, huh?" He looked as his watch. "Got some yearlings to run this morning after breakfast—" He glanced at the picture again. "Sure. There should be time."

"Good." Hannah came over and slapped him on the back. "As long as you're goin' ta town, I need a few things from the Piggly Wiggly."

Shane rolled his eyes at her. "You know I'm no good at shopping."

"But Jenny is." Essie interrupted. "She loves grocery shopping. She cooks for a living."

Shane slanted his head at her with a cocked eyebrow.

"Really! She's an excellent cook. She taught me everything I know."

Hannah started to chuckle, then stooped over the counter and wrote a list of what she needed. Shane looked as though he were trying not to, but he smiled at Essie and she smiled back.

She knew she'd been the brunt of endless jokes about her cooking. And who could blame them? But wait till they met Jenny and tasted her culinary skills. Knowing Jen, she'd probably insist on making something for tonight. Soon they'd be swallowing those smirks.

When Shane retreated to the dining room, Hannah straightened from the counter, a hand pressed to the small of her back.

"I got some beds ta change and bathrooms ta clean. Think ya can hold down the fort here without me?"

Essie watched her a moment, seeing the pain in the older woman's face. "I could do those things after I'm done here. If you're not feeling well—"

"Who says I ain't feelin' well? Jes a little lumbago. Besides, there's too much ta do. Shane's old room needs hoein' out for yer friend—"

Essie waved her hand. "Don't bother with that, Hannah. Jenny can stay with me. We have a lot of catching up to do."

"Humph. Well, there's still young Ryder. He called and said ta be sure his rooms get fresh linens...and flowers, no less." She shook her head. "Don't like the sounds a this. Not at'all." She rubbed her back again and eyed Essie. "I think I remember why that Maddy sounds familiar...it ain't good." Worry pinched deeper lines above her brow. "It ain't good, I tell ya. Not for my Ryder, leastways."

She waddled toward the west wing still shaking her head, leaving Essie with her thoughts. It sounded as though Maddy and Billy would be staying overnight. She poured orange juice and searched for a comfortable answer to the sleeping situation. Maybe Ryder planned to stay in Shane's old room or at Buck's cabin behind the stables.

Maybe pigs will fly, too.

No. She wouldn't indulge this line of thinking today. Jenny was coming and all would be well. She couldn't wait for the day to end so she and Jen could run upstairs and have one of those long heart-to-hearts she so desperately needed. Nothing Ryder could say or do would spoil tonight.

Jenny scanned the happy faces of friends and family who waited at the gate, wondering how she'd ever find Shane.

Savannah had said he was over six feet tall, and that his hair and eyes were dark like her own. She'd said he'd be wearing a cowboy hat, too.

Great! That narrowed the field by half. She stepped out of the way of traffic and removed the heavy carryon from her shoulder, setting it on the floor beside her. The crowd was thinning, with many heading for baggage pickup. Systematically, she started at the far left and looked at each remaining tall male of about thirty-two. About two-thirds of the way across she made eye contact with a handsome and somber cowboy. He was alone, leaning against a wall, his arms and ankles crossed. His gaze was fixed on her, and his expression didn't change when she met it. He neither smiled nor frowned, simply stared at her, sizing her up. For what? Whether or not she was worthy of a ride back to Joeville? She picked up her bag and walked toward him, seeing no other possible fit. When she was a yard in front of him, she jutted out her chin and shot him a bugged-eyed look, mocking his constant stare.

"Well? Are you Shane?" At last she was rewarded with something resembling a faint smile.

He touched his hat by way of greeting. "I am if you're Jenny."

"And if I'm not?"

"Then I won't have to be so polite." His smile widened only marginally as he glanced at the photo in his hand and then back to her face. "Hmm," he said, studying her features.

"Hmm, what?" What was the big deal here?

"Thought you were tanned by the photo, but that's your skin color. You're part Indian, aren't you?"

"Not by choice." And not that it was any of his business.

He eyed her critically, then took her bag off her shoulder and said, "That's too bad." He turned and started down the long corridor.

Jenny watched him amble off with a slow and soundless

gait. Too bad what? That she was part Indian or that she resented it? She shrugged, deciding it didn't matter. "Welcome to Montana," she muttered under her breath, then caught up with him a moment later.

Essie heard the loud thud and a howl that sounded like an alley cat's worst encounter. She set the bowl she was drying on the counter and raced down the hall, hoping Hannah had simply stubbed her toe or something less severe. Max hurried from the opposite direction and beat her through Ryder's door. Essie followed, worried what they might find.

Hannah knelt next to Ryder's bed, a cheek resting on the unmade sheets, beads of perspiration on her forward.

Max hunkered down beside her. "Can you stand, Hannah?"

She glowered at him. "Now, Maxwell, do ya think I'm jes resting here a bit?" She tried sounding her crusty old self, but it didn't fool either of them.

Max looked over his shoulder at Essie. "If you get the other elbow, I'll take this one. On the count of three, we'll lift her to her feet." Essie moved to the far side.

"Now, how the hell are the likes of you two goin' to move a mountain like me?"

"With a lot of help from you, Hannah." He gave her a no-nonsense look, then softened. "I know it will hurt, but we need to get you in bed." He gazed over her head at Essie. "Her back goes out once in a while. But I can make her more comfortable when she's lying down. Are you ready?"

With one hand in Hannah's armpit and the other under her elbow, Essie nodded and grit her teeth.

"One, two, three."

"Aaahhhggg!" Hannah gave it all she had and came to her feet.

"Baby steps, Hannah. Turn around and we'll help you to your room."

Hannah grunted and winced, but they made the slow

journey back to her first-floor room near the kitchen. Once there, she sat gingerly on the side of her bed, then pivoted slowly and spread out on her back. The protests of the old box springs were drowned out by Hannah's moans.

Max found towels and rolled them expertly—small ones for under her neck, knees and ankles, and a larger bath towel for behind her waist. With Essie and Max taking opposite sides, they pushed and tugged each towel into its proper place, till Hannah finally expelled a long sigh.

"Much better." She kept her head straight and talked to the ceiling. "Thank ya both. And, Maxwell, I'll be havin' some of those drugs a yers now."

Max laughed. "One muscle relaxant coming up."

Essie watched him leave and wondered again if Ryder had been too hard on his father all these years. From everything she'd seen, he was a good man. Sometimes opinionated and domineering, treating his sons as though they were still boys. But nonetheless, he was good and kind, with a bedside manner that spoke volumes about his love for his chosen profession.

He spent most of his days in his clinic in the back, mending broken cowboys or sometimes just comforting a little one with the sniffles. Maybe his career had kept him away when the boys were young, but that didn't seem reason enough for the cold war she'd witnessed more than once between all of them. Except Joshua. What did Joshua know, or not know, that set him apart?

Hannah reached out and squeezed Essie's hand, ending her idle speculation. "Sorry, girl. I'm not gonna be worth squat for a few days."

Essie patted her hand. "Everything will get done, Hannah. I don't want you to worry. Jenny will be here soon and she'll pitch in."

Max returned with a pill and a glass of water with a bent straw. "Here you go, dear." He lifted her head enough to swallow, then touched her wiry gray hair. "Try to relax, Hannah. It will work much faster that way."

There was a television at the foot of the bed. Essie found

the remote control on the nightstand. "Would you like to take your mind off things for a while?"

"Sure. Nothin' like listenin' ta others' problems ta make ya forget yer own."

Essie hit the Power button, then handed the control to Hannah. "Can I get you something to eat or drink?"

"Nah, thanks. Maybe later." Hannah closed her eyes with the control resting on her chest and Max and Essie left the room.

Essie walked side by side with Max back to his clinic. She hadn't been in this area of the house since her tour the first day. The offices were empty today and Max went directly to his desk and dropped into his large leather chair with a weary sigh. He gestured to the chair across from him and Essie sat down.

"Does this happen often?" she asked.

"Not too. It's probably been a year since the last time."

"But she'll be okay?"

Max laughed. "Hannah will outlive us all, Essie. She'll have to stay put for a few days, but she'll be fine. Trouble is, she never takes time off to simply relax and enjoy herself." He gave a self-deprecating chuckle and swept his arm across the piles of paper on his desk. "I should talk. Look at this mess. I spend every day in here and rarely put a dent in it."

Essie took in the room and his desk as if seeing it for a first time. There were shelves stacked with magazines and journals, with more piled on the floor in the corner. File cabinets lined one wall, but she didn't see any labels on drawers and wondered if he knew where anything was. Or was it all on his desk? This man needed a good secretary. In no time at all she could have this place whipped into shape and...

"Essie? I can see those wheels turning. What are you thinking?"

She sprang out of her seat and started pacing the area behind the chair. Yes. With Jenny here, it could work. She never thought she'd hear herself say she missed it, but she did. Secretarial work—organizing, typing, filing. It's what she knew best. It hadn't been the work at the warehouse she'd resented; it had been management and the grousing workers around her. This would be different.

She stopped pacing and gripped the back of the chair with both hands. If she didn't tell him now, she might lose her nerve. "I—I'm afraid I've been less than truthful with you, Max."

He leaned back in his chair and smiled, not seeming the least bit suspicious or surprised.

"Well, I—I'm not really a cook." She watched him rock back and forth and chew the inside of one cheek. "I'm sorry. I needed the job." Her deception didn't seem to faze him. If anything, he seemed amused. She forged on, realizing he seemed more interested in hearing her idea.

"I was a secretary for nearly twelve years. A good one, too."

"I'm sure you were." He smiled and stopped rocking.

"Jenny—my friend who's coming today—she's a wonderful cook." She hesitated a moment, wishing she'd talked to Jenny about this first. But it was too late. She'd started this conversation; she would finish it. Later, she'd enlist Jen's support. "I could do Hannah's cleaning…and I'd really like to tackle this office." Her gaze swept across the chaos, and she realized she probably sounded critical. "I…I mean, well—"

"You don't have to worry about hurting my feelings, Essie." He leaned forward on both elbows. "I'd love you to *tackle* this office. But do you think you'll have time?"

Excited with the prospect, she sat on the edge of the chair. "If Jenny doesn't mind cooking, I'm sure I'll find time." Besides, it would make her feel good about herself again. Between Ryder's rejection and her ineptitude in the kitchen, her self-esteem had taken an unhealthy beating lately.

Max stood, appearing a little excited himself. "Have at it, Essie. Heaven knows this place needs an experienced person." He came around the desk and placed a hand on her shoulder. "And I have no doubt you're just that person."

It was difficult to hold his gaze, but she did. "Thank you, Max." She wished she could tell him the rest of the story, but she didn't want to risk the progress she'd made. Besides, the way things stood between her and Ryder, maybe no one need ever know.

"Just one thing," he said, holding up a finger and looking suddenly serious. "Clients records are completely confidential. Whatever you see here, you can never repeat." He eyed her and waited for affirmation.

"I understand. And I promise."

He slapped her shoulder lightly, then headed for the door. "Good. Then it's settled. Start whenever you'd like."

He left her standing alone in the office. She looked at it all again and excitement danced through her. If it weren't for the party tonight, she'd love nothing better than to start right now. But there were beds to make—Ryder's. And flowers to cut—Maddy's.

She left the office, determined not to dwell on the significance of the tasks ahead. Maybe Ryder just wanted Maddy to feel welcome. Maybe they were staying overnight so he had more time with Billy. There was the paint pony in the stable. Perhaps Ryder planned to give it to Billy this weekend and that was the reason for their stay.

Whichever, it didn't matter. She returned to his quarters and finished the guest bed Hannah had started. Then she went into the bedroom that was obviously Ryder's. Evidence of Montana State University were here and there, but other than that, there were very few mementos. It was obvious now he hadn't been back here long, that he'd lived somewhere else. The pine furniture looked as though it could have been purchased yesterday. This was good, she told herself. The room didn't feel like the man, making her job easier. She snapped a fresh bottom sheet over the mattress and moved quickly to each corner, tugging the fitted white sheet into place. At the last corner near the head of bed, she saw a tiny heart carved in the headboard, two initials barely legible in the center. Curious, she stooped and read them.

"S S." Her heart pumped faster. She knelt on the floor, her face inches from the carving. She knew what she hoped to find—a year. She squinted, but saw nothing else. Just "S S."

She leaned back on her heels and closed her eyes, wishing she'd never discovered the etching. It could be anyone. How many women in the world had the initials SS? Thousands, millions. Maybe he had a thing for Sharon Stone.

Once again that little voice inside said she was lying. The more mature Ryder wouldn't have carved a heart to remember a nineties movie star.

But a teenaged Ryder might have.

She stood abruptly, willing herself back to work. What was the point of torturing herself like this? A lot had happened in the last twelve years, not the least of which was Maddy and Billy.

Billy. Could that adorable little towhead really be Ryder's son?

No. She couldn't afford this today. She had to keep moving. And the sooner she was through with this room, the better.

Shane had showered, shaved and slipped into a new pair of tan chinos and a short-sleeved purple pullover. He'd told himself it was for Ryder's party, but he knew he wanted to look nice for Jenny, though she didn't seem the type to judge a man by his cover. There was something spunky about that little gal that had amused him from the second he'd laid eyes on her. While Essie had always seemed secretive and sometimes insecure, Jenny seemed the sort to have an answer for everything, along with an attitude—one that he guessed might be masking an old anger. Yet it didn't seem to keep her from enjoying life. For miles and miles of open road, between the airport and the ranch, she'd been awestruck by the elk and antelope and mule deer, drinking it all in with a desert thirst. And unlike Essie, she looked like she belonged out here. Her darker skin could withstand the wind and sun. And those big doe eyes...

He stood at the screen door and saw Buck smoking his handmade pipe, rocking in his handmade rocker, watching the day's end. He was looking at the pass to the north, beyond which were miles of buttes and plateaus that led to the summer pasture where they would drive the cattle next week. It was one of the few times of year when Buck would leave the ranch. Shane could tell by the contentment on the old Indian's face that he was looking forward to it. Shane sat down in the matching rocker beside Buck and crossed his ankles on the railing in front of him.

"Soon...we go." Buck puffed and watched the landscape.

They rocked in companionable silence as they had for years. Shane knew what Buck would ask next, but he was in no hurry. It would be a couple of hours till dinner and there was nothing more he wanted to do than rest here with this gentle man. He wondered again how old he was. It was never discussed. Shane smiled inwardly. If he asked, he'd probably get an answer in terms of moons passed. Buck's idea of the way an Indian talked came mostly from the spaghetti Westerns that he was addicted to. He'd left the reservation long before Shane or his brothers were born, finding a job here with the horses he loved. And here he'd stayed.

"Where was the big bird from?"

Shane smiled at the predictable question and chosen words. "Detroit."

From the corner of his eye, Shane saw the slow turn of Buck's head.

"Bad Cook from there, too."

"Jenny said neither of them lived there...it was the closest airport."

"Ann Arbor, then?"

"No." Ann Arbor was probably the only other Michigan city Buck had heard of—the place Max had taught surgical students during a three-year hiatus from a troubled marriage. "No, some other place. Waterford, I think she said."

"Hmm. Probably many Fords and no water."

Shane laughed, but then fell silent when he heard excited voices racing behind the stables and moving toward the open fields. He knew Buck was waiting and watching, too, as Jenny and Essie sprang into view.

Shane and Buck rocked and watched the pair frolic in the wildflowers, playing like a pair of schoolgirls, their laughter carrying far across the fields.

After a while Buck said, "This Waterford...must be a poor village."

"Why's that?"

He wagged a gnarled finger at the girls, who were walking toward them, and then to his stomach. "Not enough thread. Tops don't meet bottoms. They wear little sisters' clothes. And shorts. Look how ragged."

Shane chuckled softly. "That's the style, old man. They buy them new that way."

"This Waterford strange place."

Shane laughed but was distracted by Jenny's smile as the women neared the porch. She lifted a huge bouquet of blue flax and camas, with shoots of yellow aster and more white daisies than she could carry. She dropped a few, but didn't stop to retrieve them. Instead, she shoved the whole bouquet into Essie's hands. He listened to them squabbling over who would make the presentation as they playfully nudged each other up the steps of the porch.

Essie held out the flowers to Shane with a timid smile. "Thank you for picking up Jenny at the airport this morning."

Shane took the flowers, dropping a few more in the process. "You're welcome." He wanted to add, "the pleasure was all mine," but he held onto that sentiment, guarding it for the right time.

"You killed them," Buck said sternly.

Stunned, the women turned to the old man who glowered at them.

Shane shuffled his feet, embarrassed by Buck's lack of finesse. "He means the flowers."

Essie looked down, but Jenny folded her arms and leaned against the railing, the same belligerent look on her face as when Shane had asked her if she were part Indian. "Not if you own a vase," she said, her chin a notch too high. The two eyed each other longer than was comfortable for Shane. He was about to say something when Buck finally spoke.

"We put them in water," he said. "But tomorrow...or next day...they die. Left with their roots they drink for weeks." He got out of his rocker and started for the door.

"Oh, Buck!" Essie called after him, and he hesitated at the screen, his back to her. "Hannah said to be sure to ask you to join us tonight."

"Tell Hannah another time." He went inside and Shane knew he wouldn't come out till they were alone again. He also knew Buck would never sit at the Malone table with Max. The pair always spoke to each other civilly, but they never ate at the same table. And this he couldn't blame on his father. He knew it was Buck who always refused.

Shane turned back to Essie and Jenny. "I'll put these in water right away. Thank you." His gaze fixed on Jenny's big brown eyes.

"We have to get back to the kitchen," Essie said, tugging at Jenny's hand. Then she smiled broadly. "Wait till you taste dinner tonight!"

Shane refrained from voicing any reservation on the subject and simply smiled back as the pair departed hand in hand. He watched Jenny's slender swagger a moment longer, and then, with a smile that wouldn't quit, he went into the house in search of a vase.

Tonight's dinner would be most interesting. First, Ryder bringing Maddy, which ought to be enough in itself to stir the pot. And now Jenny, too. *Interesting* didn't begin to describe the night ahead.

Eight

Essie and Jenny had showered and changed into black pants and blouses, topping them with starched, white frilly aprons they'd found buried in the linen closet. They'd decided to play their roles to the hilt tonight, serving these cowboys in a style they were certainly unaccustomed to. It would be a game, Jenny had said. It could be fun and take Essie's mind off Ryder and Maddy. By tacit agreement, they were saving the gory details of the last week for later tonight, when they would be alone and unrushed.

In Ryder's room, Essie arranged Sego lilies, bitterroot and some greens she'd cut herself. She looked at her watch: 5:50 p.m. They should arrive anytime. She stepped back and studied the flowers, making a small adjustment with fingers that shook. Enough of this room. She'd go help Jenny with the hors d'oeuvres.

The kitchen never smelled better. Spread on the chopping block were trays of little quiches hot from the oven, with stuffed mushroom caps ready to go in next. Per Max's instructions, wine and champagne bottles stood chilling in buckets of ice for the special occasion. Essie inhaled deeply, the aroma of onions and cheese and twice-baked potatoes making her stomach growl. Maybe she could talk herself into eating tonight after all.

"Oh, Jenny. They're going to be so surprised. Everything looks and smells so yummy." She crossed to her friend and gave her a sideways hug. Jenny broke a canapé in half and slipped a piece in Essie's mouth and ate the rest herself. "Mmm." Essie marveled at her friend, who appeared right at home in an area of the house Essie guessed would always feel alien to her.

"Wish I had one of those tall chef's hats," Jenny said. "Wouldn't that be a hoot?" She laughed as she washed her fingers then went to work on a salad that looked like a meal in itself.

Max pushed through the dining room door and stopped just inside. He wore a button-down, striped shirt, open at the collar, dress trousers and an expression that said he was obviously impressed. "I can't believe my eyes!" he said, hands on hips, taking in the scene. "Essie...you told me your friend could cook, but this promises to be better than any caterer I could have hired."

"That's because she *is* a caterer. And the best, I might add." Essie felt as proud as she knew she sounded. At last the family would have a good meal, a great meal, and without Hannah's help, even. "Max, this is my very best friend, Jenny Moon." She stepped back and let Max pass in front of her. "Jenny, this is Max Malone...Ry—I mean Shane's father."

Jenny dried her fingers and the pair shook hands.

"Jenny met Shane this morning. He was kind enough to pick her up at the airport. Good thing, too, with Hannah laid up—" She knew she was babbling, but the closer it came to the time of Ryder's arrival, the more harried she felt. "Oh, speaking of Hannah. While you two get acquainted, I thought I'd take her some of Jenny's hors d'oeuvres." Hurriedly, she fixed a plate, grabbed the tray she'd used earlier for lunch and rushed around the corner.

Hannah had rolled on her side and seemed better than the last time Essie had checked.

"'Bout time ya brought me some of those. My mouth's been waterin' fer over an hour." She popped a small quiche between her lips and her eyes widened. "Mmm-mmm, that's good." She took another.

"Do you think you're up to some supper when it's ready?"

"Does a cow like her udders rubbed with salve?" She licked her lips and gave Essie a rare smile.

Any other time, Essie would have laughed, but hearing the swell of voices coming from the living room made her chest contract, and all she could manage was a weak smile. "I'll be back as soon as I can." Hannah nodded and kept eating.

Essie raced back to the kitchen, wishing she could retreat to her apartment instead. "Jenny...I think they're here." She paced in front of the chopping block. "I don't want to be nice to him." She crossed her arms and pulled them tight to her aching chest. "And I certainly don't want to be nice to that—that *woman*."

"But that's exactly what you're going to do," Jenny said, tossing the salad. "Kill him with kindness. Trust me. Kindness will make him guilty and even more uncomfortable than you're feeling. You can do it."

"I...I don't know—"

"Okay, then pretend you're me." She winked as she poured homemade raspberry vinaigrette dressing over the greens. "Cop an attitude. Act a little bitchy."

Essie laughed and walked behind the counter for a bear hug. "If I had half your confidence—"

Jenny bussed her on the cheek and stepped back. "Come on. Let's pour some wine and champagne. I'll take the tray of hors d'oeuvres, you take the drinks. I can't wait to get a look at this stud you've got your panties in a bunch over."

They filled wineglasses and flutes and Essie pretended to feel better. But all her vital signs pointed to disaster. She didn't know why, but she had the feeling tonight was going to be worse than she'd expected. On one hand, seeing Ryder for the first time since they'd made love should be easier in a roomful of people. On the other, there was Maddy and Billy. She just couldn't reconcile this nagging feeling about the roles they played in Ryder's life.

Jenny led the way, holding the swinging door open with her back as Essie passed in front of her with her tray of tinkling crystal. They repeated the process through the closed French doors leading to the living room. A fire roared in the large stone open hearth, taking the chill off the cool spring night and giving the room a cozy glow. Ryder and the only woman in the room stood facing the flames. A little boy clung to her hand and Essie wanted to cry. Competing with a woman like Maddy was one thing, but toss in an adorable child, and she'd lost before she could put up a struggle. She nudged Jenny and pointed with her head. Jenny squared her shoulders and lifted her chin, signaling for Essie to do the same.

Max spotted them and came over, resting a light hand on Essie's shoulder. "Everyone...if I could have your attention."

The trio at the mantel turned, but only one pair of eyes came up to meet Essie's. Maddy's. She smiled faintly, her pale pink lips about the only color in her thin face. Her long, straight blond hair spilled artfully over her narrow shoulders. Essie forced a polite smile, then looked away, finding Shane standing near the bay window, his eyes riveted on Jenny. Seated next to him was Josh, who slapped his knees and stood, seeming as though he might be the only one comfortable with this little family gathering.

"Maddy and Billy, this is Essie." Max continued, unaware of the significance of the moment. "And this is Essie's friend who just arrived today from Michigan...Jenny Moon."

Essie watched Ryder's brows knit together at the mention of Michigan, but before she had time to worry about his reaction, Billy stepped in front of her, his small hand extended.

"It's nice to meet you, Essie." His cornflower blue eyes seemed wise beyond his years. And so sad.

"It's nice to meet you, too, Billy."

He sidestepped to Jenny. "Welcome to Montana, Jenny Moon."

"Why, thank you, Billy." She stooped and offered her tray. "Help yourself to an appetizer." He glanced over the selection, took a napkin and then made his choice.

Essie caught Maddy's tender smile lingering on Billy, and she knew she couldn't hate this woman, no matter how hard she tried. But when Ryder took Maddy's hand and squeezed it, Essie had to look away. She busied herself making the rounds, concentrating on not spilling a drop. Max took a flute of champagne, Josh and Shane chose wineglasses and then finally she paused in front of Ryder.

"The tall ones are champagne...the short, wine. Or I could get you something else if you prefer." She said all this pointing to the crystal and avoiding his eyes.

"This will be fine," he said, taking a glass of champagne, which surprised her. She never would have expected Ryder to be the champagne type. Still not looking up, she moved in front of Maddy, who also chose champagne. Billy returned to his mother's side and Essie lowered her tray.

"This one with the cherry is called a Shirley Temple. Would you like to try it? Or I can bring you a soda—" His chubby fingers retrieved the glass with the cherry.

"Thank you," he said, smiling up at her, his missing top tooth leaving a bigger gap around the area of her heart.

She couldn't help but smile back. "You're very welcome, Billy." She turned away, moisture teetering at the rims of her lower lashes. All was lost and she knew it. The fog of heartbreak cloaked her, and she started back for the kitchen, Jenny right in front of her.

"Please..." Max said to them. "Stay and have a toast with us."

Jenny blocked the exit, lowered her head and eyed Essie, forcing her to turn around.

"You two may be doing all the work tonight, but for as long as you stay with us, we hope you'll feel part of the family." He gestured for them to set their trays down, which they did. "One little cocktail won't spoil the cooks, will it?"

"No, of course not," Jenny said, handing Essie a flute of champagne and taking one for herself.

Max lifted his glass and everyone followed suit. "To Ryder...on his thirtieth birthday." Max held the glass in midair a moment, eyeing his middle son. "May this be the beginning of the best years of your life."

Essie's gaze flitted between the two men, hope for their reconciliation nudging aside the pain of her personal loss. If father and son could make peace before she moved on, a corner of her heart would feel better.

"Hear, hear," Josh said. And Ryder pointed his glass toward his father, then drank.

Billy tugged at Maddy's modest blue dress. "Can we, Mom?"

She nodded and smiled.

Shyly, Billy started to sing "Happy Birthday" and everyone joined in.

Essie mouthed the words, but her voice was lodged behind the lump in her throat. The song ended, and laughter and gibes followed, till Ryder raised his glass again and the room fell silent.

"Since we're in the toasting mode—" he squeezed Maddy's hand again and looked down at Billy "—there's another special occasion to celebrate. You'll read about it in the paper tomorrow morning, but thought you should all be the first to know."

Essie took a quiet step backward and ran into Jenny. She had to leave the room. The walls were moving closer, the air oppressive. Beads of perspiration wet her bangs.

Ryder raised the glass higher, his dark gaze leveled on

his father. "I'd like to toast my bride-to-be…and my son…Maddy and Billy soon-to-be Malone."

Essie staggered backward and Jenny's fingers pressed into her upper arm. If it hadn't been for Jenny against her back, holding her firm, she knew she would have bolted. There was no place in the world she wanted to be less than in this room, watching Ryder's family crush around the trio, best wishes and hugs going to Maddy instead of herself.

My bride-to-be and my son…Maddy and Billy Malone. Maddy and Billy Malone. Maddy and Billy Malone.

The words repeated and repeated in her head, crowding out all other thought. How could this be? Only two nights ago he…they—

Unexpectedly Ryder's eyes met hers. And held. In that brief moment she saw something she didn't understand. There was a plea and sadness in his eyes that forced the sob at the back of her throat a notch higher. What did he want from her? Forgiveness? Understanding? What words could ever explain this, make this pain go away? Billy said something to him, and he looked down.

Essie spun so quickly she felt the room tilt as though she were on an amusement ride. Except there was nothing amusing about tonight.

Jenny took her elbow and they retreated through the dining room and into the kitchen. The swinging door hadn't creaked to a stop before Essie buried her face in her hands and let loose a racking sob.

"Why? Why?" She let the tears come, knowing it was useless to fight them. Jenny offered a shoulder and Essie clung to her. "I…I should have found him sooner, Jen. I…I waited too long."

Jenny held her and let her cry till it seemed there was nothing left, then she started again. At last she sank into a chair. For once her friend said nothing. There were no encouraging words, no false pretense that things would work out.

They wouldn't. Jenny knew it. And so did she.

Essie blew her nose and sat staring into space. A timer

went off and Jenny took a tray from the oven, set it on the counter, then knelt on one knee in front of Essie.

"I'm really sorry, sweetheart." She patted Essie's leg. "Look, I can handle dinner by myself. Why don't you take Hannah a plate, then go on upstairs. You don't need to face these people right now."

She knew she should argue, but there was no fight left in her. She simply nodded and wiped her face with the tissue that Jenny pressed in her hand.

With a lingering look, Jenny motioned with her head to Hannah's room, then left with the fresh tray.

Moving seemed an impossible task. If she sat here a little longer, would the nightmare end? Would the fog clear and she would laugh with Jenny over this silly daydream she'd just imagined? She couldn't feel her limbs. Maybe she *was* asleep.

How long she sat there, she didn't know. The cacophony in the other room grew louder, till finally she pressed her hands to the sides of her head and ran around the corner to Hannah's room. She stood next to the bed, forgetting where she was, only glad the sound was dimmer.

"Essie?"

Hannah's gravelly voice cut through the shroud, bringing her around with a start. "Hannah!" She'd forgotten her tray.

Hannah patted the edge of the bed. "Come here, girl, and sit next ta me."

Essie inched her way closer to the kitchen chair pressed to the side of the bed, the one she'd used as a table earlier.

"Why, ya look like ya lost yer best friend."

Essie gazed down at Hannah's worried face and the tears came again—at first two little streaks down the sides of her nose, followed by the reservoir she thought she'd used up. She stood there, shaking and crying and not caring what Hannah might think.

With a loud grunt, Hannah pushed herself to a sitting position and held out her arms. Essie didn't need a second invitation. She knelt on the floor and buried her face in the lap of Hannah's flannel nightgown. Hannah stroked her hair and said nothing, letting Essie spill her pain without censure or question. With her chest aching and her mouth dry, she lifted her head and met Hannah's compassionate gaze.

"Ya kin tell me anything, ya know."

Essie pulled another tissue from her apron pocket and dabbed at her eyes and wiped her nose. "Y-you must be hungry." She started to stand, but Hannah clasped her wrist.

"Supper kin wait. What is it, girl? Can't ya tell me?"

Essie leaned back on her heels. "There's so much to tell—"

"Do I look like I'm goin' anywhere?"

From her position on the floor, she felt even more vulnerable, as though she were a little girl looking up at this giant. She was a kind and wise giant, though. Someone to be trusted.

"Y-you already know I'm not really a cook."

Hannah smiled and waited as Essie blew her nose.

"I came out here to find Ryder."

At this, Hannah's gray eyebrows shot up. "Maybe I should lay down fer this." Essie helped to ease her back on the mattress and adjusted the rolled towel beneath her waist. "Ahhh, there. That's better." She pointed to the chair beside her, and Essie sat down. "Now come on. Tell me."

"We went to high school together...in Detroit."

"Ryder never said—"

"He doesn't remember...I mean...I look a lot different and he doesn't recognize me." Now that the story had started, she felt a measure of relief, and the words tumbled out quickly.

Hannah sucked in air with each new revelation, her eyes wide and her hand covering her open mouth.

"Then when he kissed me a few days ago—" she sniffled and decided to stick to a censored version "—I thought he cared about me, too. I was going to tell him who I was, but he's been away ever since."

"But Essie...you kin still tell 'im. Maddy will be gone and—"

"No!" She hadn't meant to shout the word. "She won't be going...or if she does, he'll go with her."

"What aren't ya tellin' me, girl? Spit it out."

She looked at the old woman's face and knew she would hear it sooner or later. It would hurt her, too, yet she had to finish what she had started. She picked up Hannah's hand and held it, feeling a firm squeeze as way of encouragement.

"Ryder and Maddy—" she took a deep breath and said it quickly "—they're engaged. And they have a son, Billy."

"No!" Hannah started to sit, but fell back against the pillow with a groan. "Oh, no. Not my Ryder." Essie saw a glassy sheen come over Hannah's eyes and her own vision blurred again. After a while, Hannah whispered. "I wanted so much more for that boy." A single tear trickled down the side of her face, and she swiped at it. "Ever since his mama died...he's been so lost." She shook her head slowly from side to side. "This ain't right, Essie. A child is no reason ta marry. Besides, I cain't believe he had a son all this time and never told no one." She clung to Essie's hand, seeming to need the support as much as Essie.

Then she turned her face and stared up at Essie as though seeing her for the first time. Slowly she placed her free hand atop the other and nodded. "One mistake don't justify tother. It might take some time, Essie girl, but that boy will come ta his senses. Mark my words. He'll never marry that woman. I kin feel it in these tired ol' bones."

"Hannah—?"

"Hush, now. When was the last time ya won an argument with me, heh?"

Essie forced a small smile, trying to cheer Hannah as much as herself. "Never, Hannah."

"Then we'll jes have ta wait an' see, won't we." She patted her hand again with more conviction. "Jes ya wait an' see."

* * *

Essie was dozing when Jenny slid beneath the covers of their queen-size bed. With numbing difficulty, Essie turned over and faced her friend.

"How you doing, sweetheart?" Jenny slid closer and stroked Essie's arm.

She blinked a couple of times, too tired for the long talk she'd hoped they would have tonight. "I told Hannah who I am and about Ryder's announcement."

"How'd she take it?"

"She was very sweet to me. Don't let that crusty exterior fool you." She rolled on her back and sighed to the ceiling. "She's not too happy about Ryder and Maddy, though. She tried to convince me it was a mistake...that Ryder won't go through with it."

"She might be right."

Essie turned her head and eyed her friend. "Is this one of your clairvoyant things or just something to cheer me up?"

Jenny flopped on her back and laced her fingers behind her head. "I don't know. But something's not right with those two. Didn't you notice?"

"I didn't notice anything. After the announcement, everything was sort of a blur. Why? What did you see?"

"Well...he was kind to her. Kind, not affectionate. He paid far more attention to Billy. And Maddy! She looked sad all night long, not like someone about to be married. She rarely looked at Ryder, but often I saw these long wistful looks at her son." Jenny turned back to Essie. "Didn't you see how gaunt she looks? She barely ate a thing."

Essie had noticed Maddy's thinness. Yet what did it matter? Ryder planned to marry her, and they had a son. That was all that counted. A son. It seemed impossible. She'd always hoped his only children would be hers. She pushed the pain aside, deciding she'd had enough for one night.

"Jenny...about dinner. You worked so hard, and it's your vacation—"

"Shhh. Not another word. I loved every minute of it. Besides, we're together and that's what counts."

"I wanted to tell you all about Ryder tonight, but—"

"When you're ready." Jenny scooted closer, stuck an elbow into the pillow and propped her head up with a fist. "Want to hear about the dinner talk?"

Essie smiled and blinked hard to hold back more tears. "I'm so glad you're here. I've missed you."

"Yeah, me, too." She rearranged her pillow, looking embarrassed over all the fuss. "They're moving cows to this other pasture on Monday. A real honest-to-goodness cattle drive. Shane said we could go along if we think we can stand three days in the saddle and camping under the big sky. Of course, we'd get the job of trail cooks, but sounds like fun, don't you think?"

It did...if it weren't for the fact Ryder would be there. She was about to say that when she heard shouts from outside.

Jenny turned off the light on her nightstand and sprang from the bed. She cupped her hands around her eyes and pressed them to the window. "Can't tell for sure, but looks like Max and Ryder." She looked to Essie and started to ask something, but then knelt on the floor and pried the old wooden window up a few inches. The voices carried clearly through the narrow opening.

Essie slipped from the covers and knelt beside Jenny. She started to tell her they shouldn't be listening, but Jenny held a finger to her lips.

"How could you have been so careless with a woman like that? And then compound your mistake by saying you'd marry her? Have you lost your mind?" Max shouted, his fists on his hips, leaning in toward Ryder.

"Oh, I suppose I should just sleep with a few of them," Ryder shouted back.

"It would be a whole hell of a lot better than marrying one!"

Ryder folded his arms and didn't back off. "Maybe I should marry a nice girl, then visit the Purple Palace on the side. Have my cake and eat it, too...like you did, *Dad*."

Max stalked a few paces away and muttered. "You think you know everything, don't you?"

"I know you turned your back on Mom, and now she's dead—"

Max stalked back. "And that's my fault, right? How long am I supposed to pay for your mother—"

Ryder leaned into his father's face. "Till the day you die." He spun and headed for the stables.

Max looked after him a moment, then hung his head and stood alone on the gravel driveway. Essie rested her head on Jenny's shoulder, the heaviness in her chest worse than before. She wanted to shout out the window, "Go after him, Max." He may have made mistakes, but she knew he loved his sons. Maybe Ryder the most. She heard the screen door squeak and then bang shut. She looked out the window again and Max was gone.

Jenny closed the window on the cold night air, and the pair shivered as they tiptoed back into bed. "See?" she whispered.

"See what?" Essie whispered back.

"It doesn't look like Ryder's sleeping in Maddy's bed tonight. Strange for a couple who plan to wed and who already have a child, don't you think?" Jenny punched her pillow and rolled over. "A little late for them to be saving themselves for the wedding night."

Essie lay staring into the darkness for hours, listening to Jenny's rhythmic breathing and waiting for the door downstairs to open and shut again. Finally, when it didn't, she slipped into a light sleep, hoping, praying that the night would pass without another sound. Why his sleeping with another woman tonight mattered, after all she'd learned earlier, she didn't know. Yet somehow it did.

Nine

Jenny was in the shower when Essie pulled herself out of bed and staggered to the closet for something to wear. How was she going to do this? How many meals would she serve with Maddy and Ryder at the table?

Jenny came out of the bathroom, towel-drying her hair. "I have an idea."

Essie dropped on the side of the bed, a fresh pair of jeans and a T-shirt slung over one arm. "How can you even think at this hour of the morning?"

Jenny ignored her surly mood and started dressing. "I'll take care of breakfast, you take care of Hannah. Then if no one's around while we're cleaning up the kitchen, you can tell me about…about your week."

Essie trudged to the shower, ruffling her friend's wet head as she passed. "It's a deal."

After her second cup of coffee, Essie entered Hannah's room with a tray and a thin smile. "Feeling any better today?"

"Now, do I look like I am?" Hannah was her usual

grumpy self. With what looked like great difficulty, she raised herself higher on her pillow.

"I'm sorry—" Essie started.

"Oh, me, too." Hannah patted the side of the bed and Essie sat gingerly. "Wanna watch church service with me this mornin'? There's a pretty good preacher on channel four."

Essie tried to sound enthused. "Sure, why not?" It came out more like "What choice do I have?" Really. What choices did she have? She could go out to the dining room and wait on the newly engaged couple and their son, or she could pack her bags and leave the ranch. As long as Jenny was here, leaving wasn't an option.

So church it was.

Jenny served breakfast and made a point of telling Max that Essie was taking care of Hannah. Max nodded, looking distracted by his own problems. Ryder looked as though he hadn't slept all night, and Maddy was more pale than yesterday, which seemed impossible. Her skin was almost translucent.

Jenny refilled Maddy's teacup just as the woman pushed her chair back and started to stand.

Ryder held her chair and looked concerned. "You all right?"

"I...I just—" She slumped to the floor before Ryder could catch her.

Jenny backed away, holding the boiling water high and away from Ryder, who scrambled behind the chair and lifted Maddy in his arms.

Max was right behind him. "Take her into the clinic."

Maddy didn't open her eyes as the men raced down the hall. Jenny stared after them not moving till she heard the soft whimper behind her. Billy's chin was on his chest, and he was struggling to retain control. No one was eating anymore.

Shane was the first to move. He stood and walked to

Billy's side. "There's a new foal in the stable I need to check on. Want to go with me?"

He looked up at Shane, eyes brimming with tears. "But Mama—"

"Your mama's getting good care, Billy. Let's give them a while alone while we check on the horses. Okay?" He pulled out the boy's chair.

Billy gazed in the direction his mother had left, then stood and followed Shane through the swinging door.

All that remained was Jenny and Josh, who simply stared at each other. Finally Jenny poured herself a cup of coffee and sat down opposite him. "What do you think is the problem?"

Josh shook his head. "I haven't a clue. First the big announcement and now this. What do you make of it?"

She assumed he meant the fainting, not the engagement. She'd save her comments on that for another time. "I think Maddy is one very sick lady. She doesn't eat enough to keep a bird alive. Did you notice?"

"Yes, I did."

Jenny shrugged then sipped some coffee. "I don't know...but something is definitely wrong."

Maddy lay on the examining table, her blond wig askew from the fall. Ryder straightened it, knowing how embarrassed she'd be when she woke up.

If she woke up.

He watched his father listening to her chest through his stethoscope and wondered if this was her time. The thought flitted across his mind that next weekend's wedding might never happen, a thought that brought relief and guilt in one fell swoop. God knew he didn't wish her dead, yet he knew the time was near. Either way, Billy would have the father he deserved. This morning's paper already listed him as Billy Malone—a piece of gossip that would send tongues wagging, but would also give Billy a fighting chance at school and in this small town.

Marriage might have helped make custody incontestable,

but the closer the day, the more he wondered if he weren't doing Maddy a disservice. She knew he didn't love her. A little voice in the back of his head said, "Who are you kidding?" It wasn't Maddy that was gnawing at him. It was Essie. Sweet, innocent, vulnerable Essie. What must she be thinking? And rightfully so. It didn't matter who initiated the other night, nor that he was feeling vulnerable, too. She had no way of knowing what was ahead of him, what he must do. But he did. And he still let it happen. How could he ever explain or hope to make it up to her? If only he had waited till later, then maybe...

Max removed his stethoscope. "Has this happened before?"

Ryder refocused on Maddy's face, tucking away his memories of Essie and the look of shock and despair on her face when he'd made his announcement. "Not with me, but I'm sure it has."

Max brushed Maddy's hair away from one ear and was about to stick an instrument in it when her wig slipped backward, exposing short little stubbles on her otherwise bald head. Ryder gently coaxed it back into place, feeling his father's curious stare.

"What's this about, son?"

Ryder looked away. "It's from the chemo."

"For—?"

He expelled a long sigh, knowing there was no point concealing the truth. "Leukemia."

After a thick silence, Max asked, "Have they tried finding a bone marrow match?"

Ryder glared at him. "She says they have, but she doesn't have insurance. Do you honestly think anyone cares about a woman from the Purple Palace?"

Max felt Maddy's forehead and didn't answer. "First or second round of chemo?"

"Second."

"You wouldn't happen to have her medical records?"

Ryder let out another pent-up breath, glad he'd insisted

on her bringing them with her. "They're in my room. I'll get them."

"Wait."

Ryder stopped and turned back.

"You knew this...yet you planned to marry her?"

"I wanted Billy to have a last name, a father." He could see the question in his own father's eyes, but he wouldn't give him the answer he wanted. It was none of his business whether Billy was really a Malone. That was his last name now...or at least it would be soon. "Everyone calls him Bordello Billy behind his back. I wanted more for him." He slapped the doorjamb and went for the records, the swelling at the back of his throat making it impossible to say more.

Poor Billy. Poor little Billy.

He heard the TV preacher coming from Hannah's open door and he tilted his head to the heavens. Please, Big Guy. I know I haven't earned any favors, but help me find the words to tell Billy...when the time comes.

He found the folder in Maddy's suitcase and skimmed through the most recent entries, dropping to the bottom of the last page, dated six weeks ago. She'd told him she didn't have long and now the record confirmed it.

Months. At most.

Max raised the head of the hospital bed slowly. Ryder watched from a distance, grateful the saline and morphine dripping into the back of Maddy's left hand had helped. He thought Billy clinging to her right hand was equally responsible for her rapid improvement. For a while Billy had been spared the dreaded hour.

Max checked her pulse and asked, "Feeling better?"

"Much. Thank you." She smiled, and her gaze shifted to Billy. "Tell me what you've been doing while I've been sleeping the day away."

"There's a new foal in the stable. He's real cute, Mama. His legs look like stilts, and he's real wobbly."

Maddy chuckled softly and swept a stray lock of blond hair back off his forehead.

"And guess what?" His eyes went wide with excitement.

"What?"

"Ryder gave me the paint pony...you know, the one I told you he let me ride whenever I visited the stables with him?"

Maddy looked at Ryder leaning against the doorway, and he shrugged as if it were no big deal.

"Got too many horses to take care of, anyway. Billy's just taking one off our hands."

Billy ran back to him and hugged him around the waist. "I'll do it all by myself. You'll never have to remind me." He gazed up with his big, cornflower blue eyes and Ryder had to swallow hard. "You just wait and see."

Ryder returned his hug, then nudged him back toward his mother. The boy knew she'd been sick for some time. He'd probably figured she wouldn't get better. He was a smart little kid. But he was still a little kid.

How would he deal with the loss of his mother when the time came? God forbid that it should haunt him the rest of his days like—

Ryder leaned his head against the woodwork and closed his eyes, trying to block out the image of another time. Maddy's death would be different. There wouldn't be the gruesome discovery he'd lived with all these years. Sometimes it seemed as though it had happened to someone else, that it was a story he'd heard on the news about some woman who had bled herself to death in a bathtub. Then other times, like this, he remembered the truth.

It was his mother.

A paramedic hunkered down beside him in the hall outside the bathroom.

"Is anyone else home, son?"

Josh was in grade school and Shane in high school. Both got out later than junior high. He was always first home. Mom knew he was always the first. How could she—

"Where can we find your dad?"

Dad. When was the last time he was home? Was he even in town? He wasn't sure. "At the hospital, maybe. Number's on the refrigerator...next to the phone."

"Why don't you come out to the living room, son? I'll get you something cold to drink—"

"No!" *No. He was cold enough. Besides, he couldn't move. His eyes were closed. They had been ever since... If he didn't move, maybe he'd wake up and it would all go away.*

He felt so alone, abandoned. He'd loved her so, and she was always there. Even when everyone else was gone—if Hannah or Buck had chores that took them away—she would be waiting to hear about his day, to give him her fragile hugs, a peck on the cheek.

This couldn't be true. It was just a bad dream....

Billy tugged on his arm. "Can I? Please?"

Ryder blinked and saw his father hanging a new bag on the IV stand, and the present rushed back. He looked down at Billy. "Can you what?"

"Go on the cattle drive with you?" Behind him, Maddy was shaking her head with a plea in her eyes.

"Not this time, guy. Maybe next year...after you get used to your pony."

"Aw, gee—"

"Besides, I don't think I'll even be going this time." He couldn't leave Billy alone.

Max adjusted the drip and didn't look up. "I'll stay here with Maddy and Billy, if that's what's holding you up."

"Ryder—" Maddy waited for him to come to her side. "I want you to go. I'll be fine."

He held her gaze, trying to read more into her words. He thought he saw a promise in her eyes that she would still be here when he got back. But could she know such a thing? The report that said "Months...at most" was written weeks ago. Did weeks or days still remain?

"I don't know. Not with Hannah in bed, too." *What if*

Dad were down the hall and Billy was alone at his mother's bedside when—

Max came around the foot of the bed. "Maybe Essie will stay with Hannah. I know your brothers could use your help." He rested a hand on Ryder's shoulder and looked him in the eye. "I'll see to Billy when Maddy's resting. We'll be okay here, son." Was he remembering, too? Or had that flicker of recognition in his father's eyes been a product of his imagination?

Maddy touched the sleeve of Ryder's shirt, and Max returned to scribbling something in her chart. "If Essie stays, would you ask her to come visit with me...when she has time?"

He gazed down at her sleepy eyes, wondering why she would request such a thing. She didn't know Essie, except for their brief meeting last night. He thought about making an excuse for Essie, sparing her the ordeal of facing his fiancée. Maybe she would go on the drive, anyway. Yet if she stayed behind and he went, that would solve two problems—Maddy's request might be honored, and he wouldn't have to face Essie for three nights around a campfire, her eyes boring into him, branding him with the guilt he deserved. It was a selfish thought and he knew it. He tried again.

"Are you sure you don't want me here with you?"

She smiled up at him and stroked his arm. "Please, I want you to go." When he didn't move, she added, "I know you're concerned, but don't be. You've already done more for me than I can ever repay. Everything will be okay. I promise."

As far as he was concerned, she'd prepaid for more than he had to offer. He'd never shared her bed, but she'd freely shared her shoulder and heart whenever he'd felt broken and lost. The first time he'd gone to her he'd left money on the dresser, only to sit on her bed and pour out his guts. From that day on, on the few occasions he'd visited, he would sit on the porch swing with her or take a walk. Then when some nameless man left her with a child, Ryder had spent as much time with Billy as he could, remembering his own feelings of isolation. Now he wished he'd moved back years ago, that he'd been there more often for this lonely little boy.

Max stopped making notes on his chart. "Ryder? Would you rather I talk with Essie?"

Ryder looked from one to the other, neither knowing the reason for his reticence. "No. You take care of Maddy. I'll go find her." He left the room before they could see the tension on his face.

He had no right to ask Essie for any favors, but under the circumstances, he would take her icy stares or angry words. He had them coming.

The church service had ended and an old movie was on the TV when Ryder paused at Hannah's door. Essie tucked a sheet under Hannah's chin and started to pick up the empty tray from the nightstand, when she spotted him standing there. She looked back at Hannah's face then quickly to Ryder, holding a finger to her lips. She left the tray and tiptoed out into the hallway.

"She just fell asleep. Can you come back later?" She said this to his chest, and he fought the urge to lift her chin with his finger.

"I came to talk with you."

Her head snapped up and she glared at him. "We have nothing to—"

"Maddy is very ill." She folded her arms and turned her face to the side, making it easier for him to ask the next question. "Max could use some help with Hannah. Will you stay?"

He watched the conflict behind her eyes. Being in the same house with his fiancée was probably not her first choice, but camping with him for the next three days had to seem worse.

"I suppose," she said finally. "As long as no one's expecting fancy meals."

"If you mean Billy and Maddy, Billy would be happy with peanut butter and jelly...Maddy's not eating much these days." He exhaled loudly, wishing he didn't have to say the rest. "She asked for you."

Her head whipped around. "Maddy? Why would she ask for me?"

He shook his head slowly and caught her fleeting gaze, hoping she saw how sorry he was. "Maybe she wants to thank you for the party last night...or for the way you treated Billy. I honestly don't know." He pictured Essie bent in front of the boy, offering him his special cocktail, and he could only imagine how difficult it must have been for her to smile and be gracious.

Essie stared at her feet and took her time answering. "I'll ask Jenny if she minds going on without me. She came out here to spend time with me, you know. But she's excited about the cattle drive."

"I'm sorry..." *For everything,* he wanted to add, but he didn't. Now didn't feel like the time, and she seemed in no mood to hear it.

"Okay."

"Okay?"

"Tell Max I'll stay with Hannah." She returned to Hannah's nightstand, picked up the tray and walked to the kitchen. He watched her go, wanting to follow and explain, but he turned around and headed back to the clinic and Billy.

Maddy was sitting higher in the bed and seemed more alert when he stopped at her side. His father and Billy were nowhere in sight. "Essie will stay." He realized now she hadn't said whether she would talk with Maddy. He wondered if she would. "I still don't feel right leaving you here—"

"Not to worry." She winked at him. "I probably won't be staying here, anyway. I talked to Max about taking me back to the Palace."

"Uh-uh. You're staying right here."

"Ryder Malone, just because you plan to be my husband doesn't mean you own me. If I want to go home, I'll go home."

She gave him her best no-nonsense glare, and he knew there was no point in arguing. Besides, he could understand her wanting to go home, as long as his father thought she was well enough to leave.

He nodded toward the IV stand. "What about that?"

"I'll be done with it tonight." She looked at her toes wiggling under the sheets. "If I still need help tomorrow, I'll stay. But if I feel okay, I'm going home. Now, why don't you get out of here so I can get some more sleep."

He waited for her to look up at him, but she continued to stare at the foot of the bed. "Want me to wake you before I leave?"

"Are you kidding? At four or five in the morning? That's the time for a person to be going to sleep, not to be waking up." She tugged at the sheet and snuggled lower in the bed, closing her eyes. "I'll see you at the Palace when you get back."

He stood at her side, feeling as though he ought to put up more of a fight, but wanting to allow her some dignity, too. When she didn't open her eyes again, he left the room having made a decision. After the cattle drive, he'd tell Shane and Josh he needed time off. He would stay with Maddy and Billy in the comfort of their own home for whatever time was left. He thought again of the time he had been alone when his own mother had died, and a cold chill shot down his back. There was no way he would let that happen to Billy. When the time came, he would be there.

Billy would never be alone.

"Now don't argue with me," Essie said, tugging off her jeans in front of the closet. "All you've been doing since you got here is work. I know you want to go on this cattle drive, Jen. So you're going. It's settled." She pulled a long T-shirt over her head and walked to the bed, where Jenny sat cross-legged, flipping through the pages of a magazine. Essie sat at the foot of the bed and tucked her legs under her.

"I came out here to be with you, girlfriend."

"But you're staying two weeks, right?" Longer, if she had anything to do with it. If that spark she'd seen between Jenny and Shane ignited on the trail, maybe the stay could be indefinite.

Jenny tossed the magazine aside. "Okay. You win." She stretched out on her side and propped her head up with a bent arm. "Providing you tell me all about you and Ryder right now. I'm not leaving here without hearing the whole scoop."

As eager as she had been to talk with Jenny about what happened, now she was embarrassed. She started slowly, recalling the first encounter the day she'd been hired, eventually filling Jenny in on every detail since.

Finally she braved a long look at Jenny's angry face. "I know, I know. I had unprotected sex with him." She hung her head. "I was so blind and stupid. Maddy runs a whorehouse, for Pete's sake. Who knows what I could have contracted." She thought about the sick woman in the clinic and instantly felt guilty for her angry words. She tugged at a loose thread at the hem of her nightshirt and said what else was on her mind.

"Oh, Jen. What if I'm pregnant?"

"I brought the test kit you asked for…but it's too early, sweetie. We're going to have to wait."

She glanced up. "You're really angry with me, aren't you?"

"I probably should be, but it's that big lug I'm ticked at. You were a rookie, but I'm sure *he* wasn't. If he's been messing around at—what did you call that place?"

"The Purple Palace."

Jenny rolled her eyes and sat up. "If he's been messing around at the Purple Palace, then he sure as hell should have used protection."

"You would think so, but I can't put all the blame on him."

Jenny frowned. "Another piece of the puzzle that doesn't fit. First, he doesn't look like he's in love with Maddy, or vice versa. And now this. Do you honestly think Ryder would make love to you unprotected if he'd been dipping his stick in purple ink?'' She shook her head. ''There's something wrong with this picture.''

Essie giggled.

''What?''

''Oh, you. Just the way you talk, the way you look at things.'' She smiled at Jenny. ''It's so good to have you here.''

''Yeah, right.'' She waved a dismissive hand, then said. ''Now…I've waited long enough.'' She squirmed a little, then grinned. ''Tell me about Shane.''

Essie arched a curious brow. ''You tell me. Good trip here from the airport, or has more happened I should know about?''

Jenny shrugged. ''The airport thing was all right…except at the gate. He made some smart remark about me looking like an Indian.''

''Well—''

''Yeah, yeah. I know. But just because I'm a half-breed, doesn't mean I like it.''

''Did you tell him that?''

''Sort of.''

''Bet that went over well.''

''How was I supposed to know he lived with an Indian?''

''Jenny, Jenny. What am I going to do with you?''

She wiggled her eyebrows up and down in that Groucho Marx way of hers. ''The question should be 'What am I going to do with Shane…for three nights under the stars?' ''

Essie flopped down on her side and laughed, not missing for a heartbeat the fact that her friend hadn't mentioned whatever moments she and Shane had shared since the airport. Jenny was a far more private person than she, something that had once bothered her, but she had grown to accept. Still, if anything serious developed between the pair, she knew she would be the first to know.

Ten

Jenny and the men rode out before dawn with the cattle, leaving Max with his patient, Hannah still in bed, and Essie with time on her hands.

Sleep had eluded her most of the night as she'd puzzled over Maddy. As hard as she tried to dismiss the possibility that Maddy might be pregnant, she couldn't. That would account for passing out the way she had and the thinness, too. Maybe she'd been too nauseous to eat recently.

Still, that didn't explain why the woman had asked her to visit. Surely Ryder hadn't told her about the other night. No. She shook her head. Maybe it was simply to thank her for the party, as Ryder had suggested. If that were the case, she didn't need the praise. Besides, it was mostly Jenny's doing, anyway.

After drinking half the contents of a pot of coffee and struggling with her conscience, Essie decided to skip the visit. Instead, she wandered toward Max's office, trying to convince herself she'd planned to organize his files today, anyway. Just because Maddy's records would be on the pile now, didn't mean she should stay away.

While she worked, Max popped his head in once and offered words of appreciation for what she was doing, but otherwise she was left alone with her task. As she'd suspected, most of the file cabinets were empty, so she started by removing what was there and sorting piles on the carpeted floor. When everything was filed away, she labeled each drawer, dusted all the freshly exposed surfaces and plopped into Max's oversize leather chair with a satisfied sigh. Besides watering a couple of plants, there was nothing left to do for now.

Except read Maddy's file. The only one she'd left on his desk.

She sat very still and listened. Nothing. Not even the shuffling of Max's feet that she'd heard earlier on the tile floor of Maddy's room. She thought about it another moment, remembering Max's warning about patient confidentiality. Certainly he had meant whatever she saw or heard she couldn't repeat. Nothing had been mentioned about not reading papers that might be lying around. If she discovered anything sensitive, she wouldn't repeat it. Not even to Jenny.

Before she could change her mind, she pulled the folder closer, her gaze riveted on the name penned across the flap. Soon there would be a new last name—one she'd once hoped would be her own. She closed her eyes and tilted her head back, refusing to give in to another tear.

Finally she looked back to the folder, then pushed it away. With a heavy sigh, she pressed her palms against the desk and stood. Whatever was in there was none of her business. Nor could it change anything. What was done was done, and Maddy would soon be Ryder's wife.

Essie walked down the hall to the kitchen, the finality of her fate taking hold, sapping her last ounce of energy. Even her bedside visits with Hannah at mealtimes didn't cheer her, nor did they seem to eat up the clock. The hours ticked off slowly; the house was too quiet. It wasn't till five o'clock and Maddy's imminent departure that Essie thought the day would ever end.

With Max on one side and Essie on the other, Maddy started for the car and the short ride home. She'd been off the IV since last night, and she said she felt better after sleeping most of the day, but Essie questioned the woman's decision. It seemed wiser to stay put. Yet not having her in the house would be a relief, too. Essie was glad it wasn't her choice.

They were halfway to the car when a truck sped up the drive, stirring a tornado of dust. The cowboy behind the wheel jumped out and touched his hat to the women, then turned to Max.

"Sorry to barge in, Doc. My brother got kicked in the ribs pretty hard. We was brandin' cattle and—"

Max waved him over. "Bring him in, bring him in." He turned to the women and arched his eyebrows. "This might take a while. Should we wait, or do you think you could manage on your own?" He looked from one to the other and Essie suppressed a groan.

Great. Just what she needed. Quality time alone with Maddy. She felt guilty before the thought was complete. On a sigh, she nodded her head and took Maddy's elbow. They walked slowly to the car, and Billy ran up alongside.

"I can help. Lean on me, Mama." Maddy slipped an arm around his shoulder and smiled.

Essie felt another pang of guilt for her attitude. These people had done nothing but treat her with kindness. They shouldn't be held responsible for her own personal misery, most certainly not this innocent little boy. Not even Maddy, who couldn't possibly know what Ryder meant to her.

Billy opened the passenger door and slid across the bench seat, holding out a hand to his mother. Essie buckled Maddy in place and walked around the back of the car, where she expelled more air from her lungs and gave herself a good stiff lecture. She would do her damnedest to return this woman's kindness. It was a short drive to the house. She'd help her to bed with a smile and then leave. The anger she felt would be saved for Ryder.

Billy tugged at her hand. "Come on, Essie. I want to show you my room."

Maddy held his shoulder. "Why don't you wait till after supper, sweetheart? Go wash your hands." She turned to Essie. "You will stay for supper, won't you?" Suzette and the other women moved closer, offering words of encouragement.

"Oh, no. I...I should be getting back," Essie said.

"You did say you took a tray in to Hannah before we left, didn't you?" Maddy didn't seem to be relenting.

"Yes, but—"

"If it's Max you're worried about, don't. He can take care of himself."

Essie studied Maddy's face a moment, distracted by the idea that she may have been with both father and son. She certainly sounded as though she knew both men quite well. And Ryder's harsh words to his father the other night were ringing in her ears.

"Come on, sugar," Suzette said, half dragging her toward the dining room. "We got plenty to go 'round."

Essie bit back a chuckle, thinking that line probably had been well used under this roof and under different circumstances. The aroma from the kitchen helped her make a decision. She would stay for supper, look at Billy's room, then head back. Besides, she had to admit it—this place and its occupants fascinated her.

She was surprised when Madonna led the strange little family in grace, but she wasn't surprised to see Maddy picking at her food, barely making a dent. If the others noticed or knew the cause, they didn't let on. If anything, she thought she heard a forced gaiety in their voices as they bantered their way through the meal, an observation that caused her to lose her own appetite. There was something seriously wrong here, and she knew before dessert was served that her earlier suspicions had been way off base.

Maddy's illness hung over them all, an illness that was not occasion for jealousy or joy, her gray pallor and gauntness far worse than only days ago.

When the dishes were cleared, Billy found Essie's hand and led the way to his room, seeming eager to show it off. A sickening feeling trickled up from his dimpled fingers and shot straight for her heart. What would happen to this child if his mother—

Billy stopped in the doorway, and Essie abandoned her morbid thoughts. With a sudden weariness, she took in the cozy space that had been carved out for him. A bright red bed in the shape of a race car was covered with a tight-fitting blue spread that matched the plush carpet. Vivid posters, artistically arranged, covered all four walls—everything from sports figures to formula-one racing cars to horses. A little desk fit snugly under a blue-shaded window and next to it was mounted a bulletin board full of pictures and notes. Essie walked toward it, curious yet fearful what she might find. There were pictures of Billy at various ages, all but one of them alone. That one was with his mother, sitting on the porch in a white wicker swing. Essie scanned the photos again and saw Billy standing next to a stall with his paint pony. It appeared to be the most recent. But what she feared most wasn't there. There were no pictures of Ryder. Not with Billy, nor with Maddy. But whatever relief she had hoped to feel was not to be had.

"Do you like my room?" Billy asked behind her.

Much as she had tried to harden her heart when they'd first met, she couldn't resist liking this little gentleman. She turned and smiled at him.

"It's a neat room, Billy. It looks like something you'd see in a magazine." This made him beam, revealing the missing tooth he usually tried hard to conceal. A clamor of voices came from the area of the kitchen, and a second later Madonna was standing in the doorway, her exposed cleavage heaving with excitement.

"It's Maddy. Sh-she fainted or something," she said between gasps.

Essie pushed past her and ran down the hall, stopping when she saw the others hovered over the unmoving body on the floor.

"Call Dr. Malone. The number's—"

"We got it," Rachel said, racing for the phone.

Essie stared at the still figure, and a sickening feeling churned the contents of her stomach. "Let's put her in bed till Max gets here."

They picked her up easily, her weight even less than Essie had imagined, and followed a white-faced Billy to her room. He ran ahead and threw back the covers, his eyes wide with worry.

"Will she be okay?"

The women looked at each other and didn't answer, telling Essie all she had to know. Once Maddy was covered, Essie put one knee to the floor and pulled the boy to her.

"Max is on his way, Billy. He'll know what to do." She swallowed and watched as he bravely held a pair of tears at bay, refusing to blink.

The moan from the bed brought them both around with a start. Maddy's eyes were open and she looked disoriented, as though she were trying to figure out what had happened and where she was. Billy climbed up on the bed and buried his face in her shoulder. She wrapped an arm around him and made shushing sounds in his ear. When she looked up, it was Essie she sought and found. Essie held her lingering gaze, wondering what message she was trying to convey.

"Madonna, would you mind getting Billy some ice cream?"

"No, Mama. I don't want to leave you." He started to cry, and Maddy stroked his hair.

"Just for a while, my little man. I'd like to talk with Essie, okay?"

He lifted his head and looked at her face. "Then can I come back?"

"Yes. Then you can come back."

He stepped back tentatively and Madonna grasped his

hand and led him away, the others filing out silently behind him.

Maddy motioned for Essie to come closer, to sit beside her on the bed. Essie hesitated for only a heartbeat. It suddenly seemed clear why Maddy had insisted on coming here. It wasn't just for the comfort of her own bed. It was home. Her place of choice to die. Whatever was wrong with her, it was terminal. Essie could see it in Maddy's knowing eyes.

Essie sat on the edge of the bed and prayed that Max would arrive soon, that another IV might make the difference and buy Maddy more time.

"You don't like me much, do you?" Maddy's voice seemed surprisingly strong.

Essie looked out the window, grasping for the right response that wouldn't ring false.

"And it's not because of what I do...or did," she corrected. "It's because of Ryder's announcement last Saturday, isn't it?"

Essie looked back at the fragile but wise woman.

"I watched you watching him. And I saw him trying not to look at you."

"Maddy," she said, feebly trying to deny it. "We were only in the same room for minutes—"

Maddy reached for her hand and covered it with her own. "When you've been in my line of business for as many years as I have, you learn to read people quickly." Essie glanced down. "Look at me, Essie. It's okay." A weak smile curved her pale lips. "I have some things to tell you. Trust me...they're not bad. But I have to say them fast."

She closed her eyes and took several shallow breaths. Then, holding Essie's gaze she continued. "Ryder wanted Billy to have a last name." She looked away wistfully, her eyes sad and tired. "Ryder knew I wanted this, too—" she looked back at her "—before I died. And he knew that wouldn't be long."

Essie struggled to hold the woman's even gaze.

"Essie...Ryder and I have never...well, you know... been intimate."

Essie blinked, not believing her ears.

"We've known each other for years. In the early days he just needed a friend...someone to listen to his troubles." Maddy closed her eyes and paused. "But I know it's only because of Billy that we've seen so much of him lately. He took a shine to the boy right from the beginning."

She wanted to ask "What troubles?" But the focus was on Billy and rightfully so. Now wasn't the time, and Maddy looked so tired, her words coming in short spurts now. As if reading her mind, she offered one important clue.

"Someday, when the time is right...ask him why he's angry with his mother."

Her eyes were still closed, and Essie wondered if Maddy had made a mistake. Surely she had meant to say *father*, not *mother*.

"He's never said he was—" she opened her eyes and her eyebrows knitted together "—but I'm sure that's the key. Make him talk to you about it, Essie. He never has and he won't be whole till he does."

Essie nodded, not sure what she was hearing, but knowing for certain that one day she would learn. As she started puzzling over it, she thought of something else. If Billy wasn't Ryder's and they weren't married, what would become of the boy after—

She stared at Maddy, wondering if she was telling the truth.

"Maddy...about Billy—"

"Essie...Billy isn't Ryder's. You must believe me."

Essie could see the sincerity coming from the woman's soul, and it touched her—not just the words, but the generosity in assuring her when other things seemed far more important. A slight smile crinkled the corners of Maddy's eyes.

"Nine months before Billy was born, I had a really good week." She started to chuckle, but it turned into a raspy cough. Essie reached out for her hand and squeezed the bony fingers gently. Maddy squeezed back and regained control.

"I could hear that old biological clock ticking. And then I got this idea. I waited for just the right time of month and just the right clientele—a judge, a preacher and a scientist. Nine months later I hit pay dirt with the most beautiful little boy. I don't know who the daddy is, but I do know Billy's from a good gene pool. You can tell by talking with him, can't you?" Her face begged for reassurance, and Essie gave it easily, honestly.

"Yes, Billy is adorable and very bright." She swallowed hard. "And very well mannered. You did a good job, Maddy."

Essie fought to compose herself as a tear slid down the side of Maddy's face. Quickly the woman wiped it away, her face taking on a painful intensity as she struggled to push out the next words.

"It's all legal...we had an attorney draw everything up. Billy's last name is Malone now and Ryder's in the process of adopting him. Our being married was supposed to have eliminated any custody question...but hopefully that won't be a problem." She closed her eyes again, and Essie stared at the ceiling.

She understood it all now—the sadness in Ryder's eyes after they had made love, his staying away later, the sudden wedding plans. Maddy grasped at her hand, and Essie looked down at the shadow of a woman.

"If you love Ryder...all I ask is that you be good to my son." She waited patiently for a response, her gaze analyzing every feature of Essie's face, demanding nothing short of the truth.

Essie pressed down on Maddy's hand and tried to speak, but the words were obstructed by the pain at the back of her throat. This woman was losing more than her life; she was losing something far more precious to her—her treasured only child.

Billy came running back into the room and threw his

arms around his mother's neck. Over his head, Maddy's gaze remained riveted.

Essie whispered, "I promise."

Maddy weighed her answer, then a gentleness returned to her strained features. She grasped Billy's shoulders and held him away from her, looking as though she were memorizing every last detail.

Essie couldn't watch another second. She rose from the bed and walked to the window. The one person she had thought stood between herself and Ryder was fighting for her life.

And Essie wanted Maddy to win.

She lifted her eyes to the stars, twinkling bright in the biggest, bluest sky she'd ever seen. Was there a heaven for women like Maddy? Would she be afforded the privilege of watching over Billy as he grew? Essie wanted to believe this good woman would see it all. Behind her she listened to words that had to be spoken.

"Billy...I'm counting on you to be very brave."

He sniffed. "Mama...you're scaring me."

"I know, little man. I know." Except for Billy's sniffling, there was silence for a long moment, and Essie turned around, dreading what she might find—if not now, soon. Maddy's eyes were closed, but her chest still rose and fell. Her lashes fluttered, then parted narrowly.

"Remember those storybooks with pictures of angels?"

"No, Mama, please—"

"I'm going to go play with them soon." Billy began to cry, but she pushed on. "That's how I want you to picture me, little one. Maybe I'll even put on some wings when we play..."

Max entered the room in a flurry, a bag in one hand and an IV stand in the other. Without a word he positioned the stand, lifted a hand from Billy's heaving shoulders and found a vein. Seconds later he adjusted the drip.

"Son, would you mind waiting outside with Essie?" His look was tender but insistent. Billy kissed his mother on the cheek, and she kissed him back, wiping each of his damp cheeks dry with her free hand. He backed out of the room, his little fingers squeezing Essie's, as Maddy gave them each a long, lingering look.

Essie closed the door softly and walked Billy to the porch, where they sat on the big wicker swing in the dark and waited for Max to come out.

What seemed an eternity was in actuality less than an hour. When Max finally approached them, his steps were slow and measured. Essie looked up at him, knowing what she would find. But knowing didn't prepare her for the pain that coursed through her when she met his eyes.

Billy was now an orphan.

Max heaved a sigh and stared into the night. "I'll make the necessary calls, then I'll ride out to the pasture and find Ryder."

Billy sat rigid at her side, not looking at Max, probably wishing he weren't such a bright little boy, hoping he misunderstood what he was hearing. Nothing had been said, really. It was clear what had happened.

"Will you see to Billy?"

She peered into Max's haggard face and simply nodded.

He turned and walked inside, shutting the screen door softly behind him. Still, Billy refused to look at her. She started the swing moving slowly, deciding there was no rush to tell him, deciding he already knew.

They glided back and forth, the sound of crunching gravel under tires fading into nothingness as Max drove from sight. Eventually she slipped an arm around Billy's small shoulders and pulled him closer. He came without a struggle, resting his head on her breast. The swing lulled them into a limbo neither seemed eager to leave.

In the end it was Billy who spoke first. "Can we go say goodbye?" She felt his warm breath through the thin fabric of her top. She hugged him hard, remembering a time when she was alone with her father, right after he had died. Her heart ached for what Billy was about to endure. He was far too young. She stroked his head, smothered against her chest, and rocked him side to side. When she stood, he came with her shyly, holding her hand in his as they walked inside and went to the quiet room.

Max had left a light on beside the bed. The bulb was pink and cast a rosy glow over the creamy sheets and the woman who lay still beneath them. The muscles in her face had relaxed; the pain was gone.

Billy let go of Essie's hand and moved trancelike to his mother's side. He pulled himself onto the high, four-poster bed and snuggled atop the sheets beside her, his ear to her chest as if listening for a sound he knew wasn't there. Essie watched from the doorway, hot tears falling fast over her cold skin. She felt like an intruder, yet she couldn't leave him here alone. She listened to his little voice whispering words of love, and she hugged herself tighter, her shoulders lurching forward with a sob she wouldn't indulge. She wondered if Maddy could see and hear her son.

If she could, she would be so proud of her brave little man.

Essie was still standing in the doorway, watching over Billy, when she heard the men return. One set of boot steps approached, and she turned to meet Ryder. She tried to let him know with a look that she knew everything. He held her gaze, and she thought he understood. But for now everything paled next to the needs of the young boy on the bed. She stepped aside, and Ryder moved slowly toward him. The selfish thought crossed her mind that she was glad it was Ryder who had to separate Billy from his mother. If he hadn't come, she wasn't sure she would have had the strength to do it.

With the gentlest touch, Ryder picked up Billy. The boy reached back for his mother as Ryder stepped away from the bed. Billy wrapped his legs around Ryder's waist and flung his short chubby arms around his neck. "My m-mama, my m-mama—"

"I know, pal." Ryder closed his eyes against the pain and hugged the boy closer.

"N-now I'm all a-alone."

"You'll never be alone, Billy," he whispered over the boy's shoulder. Then he opened his eyes and caught Essie's gaze. "I'll never leave you. Don't you worry. I'll never leave you."

She thought he seemed to be saying the words to her as much as to Billy, but she knew that couldn't be. How could he be saying what her heart longed to hear? And at a time like this? It was the emotion of the moment and nothing more. The promise had been made to Billy and Billy alone.

Then she remembered the promise she'd made to Maddy just before she died. *If you love him, all I ask is that you be good to my son.*

Essie closed her eyes. That part will be easy, Maddy.

Billy was already in her heart. Whatever happened or didn't happen between Ryder and her, Billy would always be in her life.

Eleven

Except for a brief service three days later on the ridge overlooking the Purple Palace, where Maddy had requested her ashes be buried, Essie had not laid eyes on Ryder. He had decided to stay at the Palace with Billy for a while to help take care of things, he had said. In the days that followed, a pall settled over the Malone ranch. No one talked about it, but Maddy's death and the breaking of a little boy's heart weighed heavily on everyone. Even Hannah, who had resumed a few light chores, was more subdued than usual.

Jenny had insisted on doing all the cooking, so Essie distracted herself by helping Hannah with the cleaning and working in Max's office in her spare time. After meals, she would help Jenny in the kitchen, and they would talk about whatever crossed their minds.

On Sunday afternoon, ten days after the funeral, Essie worried about Billy as she helped Jenny with the dishes. She dried a large platter and thought about the women at the Purple Palace. They loved him, of that she was certain.

Maddy had left each of them equal shares of the property so that nothing would change after her death, and they would all have a home. Still, it was no place for a child to be raised. Even though it was the only home Billy had ever known, it was time he left there and began anew. She wondered why Ryder hadn't brought him back to the ranch yet. Surely he meant to. She opened a cupboard door and put the platter away.

"I can hear those wheels turning. What's going on?" Jenny handed her the last dish.

"Oh, I've just been thinking about Billy." She stopped drying and met Jenny's curious look. There was something else on her mind, which she knew her friend hadn't forgotten with the passing of time. "I'm two days late, Jen."

Jenny shrugged, acting as though it wasn't any big deal. "Could be stress...any number of things." She untied her apron and hung it on a hook behind the door. "There's one way to know. Want to go upstairs and find out?"

Essie nodded and the pair hustled up the back stairway.

Jenny was sitting in the middle of the bed when Essie came out of the bathroom minutes later. She moved slowly toward the bed, blotting her eyes with a tissue and sniffling.

"Ah, Savannah...don't cry. We'll work it out." Jenny patted the spot in front of her. "I'll help you."

Essie dropped on the bed and propped her back on a corner post. "There's nothing to work out."

"Then why the tears?"

"I didn't realize till this very moment—" she paused and blew her nose "—but I guess I wanted to..." She let her words trail off.

Jenny wiggled closer and rested a hand on Essie's knee. "Look...it's a beautiful Sunday afternoon, there's nothing left to do, and it's been long enough since the funeral. Why don't you ride over and see Ryder, talk to him."

"Some vacation this has turned out to be, huh?"

"Oh, pshaw." She gave a flick of her wrist. "I wrangled an extra week out of my boss. We got till next Sunday to play. Besides, you don't hear me complaining, do you?"

Essie studied her friend's devilish grin and knew exactly who she was thinking about: Shane. She'd heard enough about the cattle drive to know something was brewing between the pair. She also knew Jenny had taken off on a horse more than once, and she doubted that she was always alone, though Jenny hadn't said one way or the other. As much as they treasured their time together, Essie suspected Shane was the real reason Jenny had arranged for the additional week's vacation without prodding.

Jenny scooted back in the bed and fluffed a couple of pillows against the headboard. "Did I tell you Max *paid* me this morning?"

"Good! You've been working your butt off since you got here."

"I tried arguing with him, but he insisted." She settled back against the pillows and frowned. "It doesn't make sense, does it?"

"What? Him paying you?"

"No. The picture we both had of Max before we came out here. He's not the heartless workaholic Ryder painted. Do you think he could have changed that much since Ryder was a kid?"

She thought about it a moment, then shook her head. "I've wondered the same thing." Maddy's words came back to her. *Ask him why he's angry with his mother.* Could Maddy have been right? Was Ryder harboring a secret about his mother that would shed light on his anger?

"Go on, Savannah. Go talk to him." She locked her hands behind her head and grinned. "I'll find something to do while you're gone."

"If I didn't know better, I'd think you were trying to get rid of me."

She hiked her eyebrows. *"Moi?"*

"Okay, okay. I'm going." Essie checked her makeup in the mirror, then waved goodbye to Jenny.

She did a quick check on Hannah, who had fallen asleep in the middle of her Sunday-afternoon movie, and then walked outside, just as the familiar pickup drove up the dusty path to the house. She shielded her eyes with the side of her hand and noticed that the passenger seat was empty.

Ryder stepped out, and she walked to meet him, her heart pumping irregular beats. There was so much for them to talk about, not the least of which was the truth of her identity. He stopped in front of her, removed his Stetson and raked his fingers through his unruly brown hair. There were shadows under his eyes and worry etched on his forehead. When he didn't say anything, she asked the first question.

"Where's Billy?"

"He's packing up his room. I'm moving him here tomorrow. I told him I had some business to take care of—that I'd be back later." He stared at her, and her pulse raced faster. His eyes asked something long before his lips moved again. "Want to ride with me?"

She nodded slowly, and they headed for the stables. They saddled up their horses and followed the familiar trail. When they finally turned off and followed the narrow path that led down to the stream, she knew exactly where he was taking her.

A corner of his brain told him he was returning to the scene of the crime, yet crime didn't quite fit the way he felt about that night. He stole a sideways glance at Essie's face as they ambled slowly toward their destination. She seemed a little anxious, yet who could blame her? This was the place where they had both allowed themselves to be vulnerable, to act on their feelings, to be honest with each other. His conscience pinched when he thought of honesty. He hadn't actually lied to her that night. He never could, since he hated liars. His parents had taught him well the consequences of deception.

They cleared the last thicket and came along the banks of the stream. He brushed the old anger aside, convincing himself he hadn't lied to Essie. His sins were more those of omission. He had told her the timing wasn't right, that there was a lot she didn't know. Yet if he had told her the whole story, she wouldn't have made love with him and he knew it.

Ryder watched her tether her horse to a cottonwood, then walk to the stream's edge. Sun filtered through the trees, highlighting lighter shades of her hair, hair that till now he had thought was much darker. She stood watching the water rush by, rays of sun reflecting off the surface. As much as he longed to take her in his arms again, that wasn't his motivation for seeking this spot. It had more to do with telling her how sorry he was for having hurt her the last time they'd come here, and for thanking her for her kindness to Maddy and Billy.

He tied his horse and walked to her side, resisting the urge to slip an arm around her slender waist. He picked up a handful of stones and skipped one on the water instead.

"I don't know where to begin, Essie." He skipped a second stone, searching for the right words.

"Maddy told me, Ryder. She told me everything…just before she—"

The unfinished words hung in the hot summer's day, while birds sang and the water raced by, filling the silence with peaceful sounds.

After a while he said, "I should have told you more that night…so you would have known before the party." He flung a stone as far as he could. "I didn't mean to hurt you. I—I'm sorry." As difficult as it was to say the words, they now seemed far too inadequate. When she didn't say anything, he turned and looked at her. It wasn't anger he saw in her eyes and wrinkled forehead. It seemed more like confusion or anxiety. Yet if Maddy had told her everything, what could she be so conflicted about now?

"Essie…I never touched Maddy. If you're worried about—"

"No." She faced him with her eyes still cast down. "I'm not worried about that." Slowly she looked up, her eyes meeting his briefly, then skittering away. "I wanted you to make love to me, Ryder." She looked back at his face and held his gaze. "I still do."

He rested his hands on her bare shoulders, feeling the warmth of the sun on her tanned skin. "Essie…why me? Why was I the first?"

She leaned into him and answered his question with a soft kiss on his cheek, then she whispered in his ear. "It was the way God intended it, Ryder."

Why she sounded so certain, he didn't know, but feeling her pressed against the length of him left little room for doubting her words. He lifted her chin with his fingers and gazed into blue eyes that seemed as familiar as the midday sun. They were very much like Billy's, he thought, and in the next second, he wondered if their own children would have her blues or his browns. His gaze traveled to her mouth and watched her lips part ever so slightly as he met them with his own. A groan slid from deep inside him into her trusting mouth, and he knew he was lost. This is what he'd wanted ever since the first time. Not just another kiss and the feel of her body beneath him, but a lifetime of both.

He felt her arms wrap around his back as she pulled him closer, her full breasts flattening against his chest, awakening other parts of him that longed to touch her, to stroke her, to show her how much he cared.

He yearned to fill that tight little space that she'd reserved for him. The fact that it was so private a place, that she had shared it with no one but him, excited him beyond measure. Why she chose him, out of all the men in the world who surely found her attractive, who must have tried, he didn't know. Yet he was glad. For some reason it made him trust her even more, just knowing that she valued herself enough to wait for— For what? The right man? Did she think he was the right man? Did she love him? The thought was both frightening and heady, carrying with it a responsibility he hoped he could live up to.

His eyes never leaving hers, he took her hand and led her to a mossy incline and guided her down beside him. Her fingers reached up and brushed the hair off his forehead and he felt his blood pooling and thickening with a need so strong and urgent that he felt it difficult to breathe. Her chest was rising and falling, too, which forced his gaze to the tiny buttons down the front of her short white top. He felt clumsy as his big fingers worked the little buttons, and he wished he could rip them away. When the last was open, he pushed the fabric aside and she shrugged her arms free of it.

She didn't wait for him to remove anything else. She hurriedly shed the rest of her clothes while he undressed himself with lightning speed, eager to feel the warmth of his body next to hers. Gone was the shyness he'd seen in her eyes the first time. Her hunger burned and sizzled right along with his. She held her outstretched arms to him, and he lowered himself to her, willing back the explosion wanting to burst from him.

He supported his weight on one elbow and with his free hand traced the full swell of one breast, then the other, moaning as he sucked a nipple to full arousal with his lips and tongue. She groaned and writhed beneath him, spreading her legs to accommodate his knees.

When she reached down and cupped him with her warm, gentle touch, he gritted his teeth and counted to ten. He wanted this woman. Hard and fast, till neither of them could find air or energy, till they dropped in a pool of their own love and heat. The mere thought left his sex throbbing harder, painfully so.

He ravaged her mouth, leaving it red and puffy when he pulled back and looked into her face. There he saw the depth of her passion. He wanted to please her as much as he wanted to be inside her. He rose on his knees and eyed every inch of her pure and beautiful body, letting his hands trail lightly down the length of her, watching her head tilt back and eyes close. With his fingers poised at her silky entrance, he flicked a thumb back and forth over the rise at her opening, then slid a finger inside, working it in and out in a rhythm her body would recognize. She groaned a long, throaty sound and it spurred him on. He quickened his pace with his finger and thumb and her hips ground into his hand.

"Don't hold back, baby. Let it go." He rubbed harder and faster till she screamed and filled the palm of his hand with a sweet reward. Unable to wait another second, he guided himself slowly, gently inside her, resisting the urge to bury himself in her narrow inner walls. Finally she made the decision for him, lifting her hips to meet him, pulling him to her with both hands.

He rode her long and hard, her energy and need matching his every thrust. He never wanted it to stop—this oneness— this whole feeling he'd never thought existed. He lowered himself to her and claimed her mouth again, his tongue tracing her lips and every depth beyond. She held him tight, her arms locked behind his neck, sucking him closer and closer, till he thought he might drown in her. When she lifted her hips and rotated them again, he gave in to the primal urge to fill her. A chill shot down his spine and his shoulders shuddered, his flow into her a never-ending stream.

When he was spent, he opened his eyes and saw the look of love on her face, and he slumped against her, kissing her moist neck and shoulders, tasting her salt, smelling the gentle fruity scent of her perfume. He took it all in, marveling that he had gone thirty years without knowing this kind of trust and love and oneness. He kissed her cheek and tasted her tears. He pulled back and studied her face.

"Anything wrong?"

She looked up at him and smiled, her head turning slowly from side to side. He brushed a finger under each eye, then dried her face with his hands.

"You're beautiful, you know?"

Her smile widened marginally. "Am I?"

He laughed easily, then cocked his head to her. "Are you fishing, now?"

She reached up and kissed his nose playfully. "No. Just glad you think so."

"Who wouldn't?" He sat up and tugged her to his side, wrapping an arm around her waist.

She didn't answer, but stared straight ahead as a fish

cleared the water then dived back under. On a giggle, she pointed and watched, bringing her knees up and hugging them to her chest. They sat there and watched nature go about its day, nothing changing, yet everything more alive, more beautiful.

After a while, she said, "Tell me about Maddy and Billy."

Of all the subjects she could have chosen, this one surprised him. "You sure you want to hear all this now?"

"Unless you'd rather not say."

Maybe now wasn't a bad time to set things straight. He kissed her temple and began. "I was just a kid...just home from Detroit and high school graduation." She looked away, and he wondered if she was afraid he might say something she didn't want to hear, but knowing he wouldn't, he went on.

"I went to the Purple Palace on a dare from one of the hired hands." He laughed as he remembered. "Had to cash a bond my grandmother had given me so I'd have enough money without going to Dad." Not that Dad should have objected, he thought, remembering the fact that his father had gone there himself. He wondered again how many times while his mother was still alive.

"Ryder?"

"Anyway—" he searched to find his place "—I thought I was such a stud. Where I got that notion is beyond me. Must have been the football in Detroit." There it was again. The shadow that crossed over her face. "All jocks aren't as experienced as they pretend to be." Her look was distracting him, so he decided to make a long story short. "The first time I met her she asked me about my family, and I ended up sitting at the foot of her bed, fully clothed, pouring my guts out about...stuff."

"Then you never really...?" Her eyes begged for confirmation, and he gave it to her in the form of light kiss in the hollow of her neck. When he pulled back and met her eyes, he could still see her doubt.

"No, Essie. I'm not lying to you. Not to protect your

feelings. Not for any reason. That's one thing you can count on—I'll never lie to you.'' She looked up at the sun cutting through cottonwood branches and heaved a sigh. Something was eating at her, and he intended to draw it out. From day one he'd sensed she had a secret and now he wanted to know what it was. But before he could ask his own questions, she pressed on.

"And Billy?''

"Ah, Billy. You only have to look at him to see how he stole my heart.'' This brought a smile to her face and she nodded agreement. "He's the main reason I moved back here…to be closer to him, teach him things, make sure he didn't feel bad not having a dad.'' As he had felt growing up, with his father out of town or at work at all hours.

Essie sat forward. "Why did you ever leave the ranch?''

He looked away, deciding on the shorter answer. "Things were never the same here after I went to Detroit and then college.'' He could feel her even stare, and for a moment he thought she would press for more, but instead she changed tacks.

"Tell me about that best friend you mentioned the day we drove to Billings,'' she began, looking a little nervous as she hugged her knees tighter. "Then I'll tell you about mine.''

She smiled sweetly, yet he saw the sadness in her eyes. Maybe that was where the secret was sequestered—in her high school days. "Well, okay.'' He lay down beside her, locked his hands behind his head and stared at puffs of clouds floating overhead. Taking his cue, she lay beside him.

"Her name was Savannah.'' He paused and pictured her in her baggy sweatshirt and corduroy pants, her long light brown hair falling in soft waves around her shoulders, her smile a thin, close-lipped one that always fought to hide her braces. "Geez, Essie, I'm not sure what to tell you.'' He looked over at her and saw that her eyes were closed tight, the space between them pinched. Puzzled, he continued.

"She was a good friend. She listened to all my grumbling and tolerated my foul moods, especially on big game nights, when we lost. She had a pretty face, kind eyes." He squinted at the sun and thought back. "Blue. Yes, they were blue."

"Did you ever...well, kiss her or anything?"

Ryder chuckled. "Oh, yeah. Just before graduation, after the prom...well, we were going at it pretty hot and heavy, but then we stopped."

"Why's that?"

"Well, for one thing she told me she was a virgin, and I knew I would be leaving town soon. Besides—" he shook his head "—I don't know how to say this."

"Try."

He hadn't been ready to trust a woman. That was the crux of it. But at the time he hadn't stopped to analyze it. "It just didn't seem right. And...well...you'd have to know Savannah to understand." He looked at Essie and saw she wanted more. "The problem with Savannah was she didn't think too highly of herself. She wasn't thin like most of the girls back then—"

"And that made a difference to you?"

"Not to me. But it did to her. She'd put herself down all the time...called herself an ugly little fat girl. Then she'd eat another bag of cookies. It was sad, now that I think back on it. Her mother left her in the care of a neighbor when she was pretty young, after her father died. Once she said something about feeling abandoned...like no one ever really loved her." A feeling he'd understood too well. Had that been the real bond between them? There was stony silence now, and he turned to see if he'd put Essie to sleep. Her eyes were closed again and she wasn't moving.

"Go ahead," she whispered.

"I'm boring you."

"No, you're not."

"Well, there's not much left to tell. After the prom...when I stopped...well, she got pretty hot under the collar and I took her home. There was this place we used to hang out. I wasn't ready to call it a night, so I went there. Just as I was getting in my car to go home, this cheerleader we both knew cornered me. I think she'd been drinking. I don't remember now. All I remember is that she laid this big sloppy kiss on me just as Savannah pulled up alongside my car. I pushed the girl away and called after Savannah, but she laid rubber like there was no tomorrow. I tried talking to her several times after that, but she always walked away. Just before I left I called her and started to explain, and she just shouted at me that I was a liar, and she hung up. Then I moved back to Montana and that was that. Like I told you before—I might have written, but she made it perfectly clear there was no point, so I didn't.''

''If she was so important to you, why did you give up on her?'' There was a tone in her voice he didn't understand, as though she assumed it had to have been all his fault.

''I told Savannah things I never told anyone else—about my parents and their lies to put up a good front for their sham of a marriage. She knew how much I hated liars, so when she called me one, it really rocked me for some time. But you know, I kept hoping something would change, that she'd find me one day and things would go back to the way they were. You know, I always wondered if she intentionally acted angry at the end, just to drive me away. All through high school, we never fought. Oh, debated maybe, but no real fights. Then, when it's almost over, she acts like I'm enemy number one. Why, if we were really friends, would a girl do that?'' It was a rhetorical question, one he didn't expect Essie to answer. But when she sat up he could see she was struggling with the words she wanted to say.

''Maybe it hurt her too much to see you go.'' A tear teetered on one bottom lash, then lost its battle and slid down her sun-pinked face. She wiped it away, looking embarrassed. ''Maybe she thought you'd only write to her now and then out of pity...and she wanted to spare you both that." She brushed off pieces of grass and weeds from her legs, keeping her eyes focused on her hands.

"Yeah, well, maybe she was my only true friend, and I didn't want to lose her." He hadn't realized how true the words were till he'd spoken them.

"But maybe he was more than a friend to her...and she feared the day he'd write to her about falling in love...with someone else."

A late-afternoon breeze stirred the air around them, and he got a small whiff of her perfume. He inhaled deeply and smiled. "You haven't worn that scent for a while. I remember the coconut from before and—"

"I stopped wearing it till a few days ago...till I decided it was time."

"Time for what?" He picked a tall blade of grass from between his feet and played with it, enjoying this little heart-to-heart more than he thought he would. Not since Savannah had he felt this comfortable with a woman. When she didn't answer his question, he looked at her face. Her bottom lip was quivering and another tear slid down her beautiful face.

"Essie—?"

"I...I stopped wearing it because—" She sucked in air and let the rest of her words tumble out, as if they held a bitter taste in her mouth and she couldn't stand them inside another second. "I—I was afraid you would remember where you...who wore that same perfume."

He stared at her, an unknown fear swirling behind his rib cage. The perfume? He didn't understand. Essie stared back, her blue eyes boring into him, waiting. He studied her face for a clue, and she bit her bottom lip, fear and self-doubts colliding behind that heady familiar scent and those big baby blues. The sun blazed down through the trees, and when she bent her head he saw lighter roots of hair near her scalp, leaving no doubt it wasn't her true color. His head started to spin and he looked away.

Lighter hair...coconut...baby blues...she always bit her bottom lip when she felt insecure...

And this woman sitting beside him said she was from the Midwest.

He turned on her, his blood pumping faster, his temper barely in check. "Is this some kind of sick joke? Who are you? How do you know so much about Savannah?" The obvious was impossible to believe.

"Ryder—" A steady stream of tears trailed down her cheeks now and she did nothing to hide them. "I wanted to know you as a man...to see what you were like...if you were involved with someone else or still free—"

He sprang to his feet, his chest heaving. Either she had befriended Savannah and was acting out some bizarre fantasy...or...or...

He stalked back to within inches of her and glared down. He clenched his fists at his sides to keep from pulling her to her feet and shaking the truth from her. "Who are you?" he asked between clenched teeth. She stood and stumbled backward. He caught her and tightened his grip on her arms. "Tell me, damn it. Tell me now."

"Don't you know?" she asked, pleading once again with her eyes.

"Tell me!" he shouted. He saw her flinch, but she didn't back away.

"S. E. Smith," she said, raising her chin a notch, her mouth still quivering.

"Don't give me this Essie crap—"

"I didn't say Essie. I said S. E. Smith." She enunciated the initials and held his gaze, searching his face as if she were waiting for the light to go on behind his eyes. "Ryder...what was Savannah's middle name?"

"How the hell do I know?" He tried to remember, impatient with this woman's game.

And then the light went on.

She looked up at him as his face registered the shock. "Elizabeth?" he asked. She nodded slowly, and he dropped his hold on her and staggered backward.

"I had to do it this way. Don't you see?" She took a step forward and he backed away. "I didn't want you feeling obligated to be nice to me." She kept walking toward him, but he didn't stop. "Ryder, please. You have to understand. I wanted to see if you could truly love me...as I've always—"

"Enough." He pushed a stiff arm to her shoulder, keeping her a safe distance. "I understand enough, Essie...or Savannah...or whatever you want to call yourself. I understand you lied and deceived me every step of the way— starting in Detroit when you wouldn't talk to me, and now this." He gave her his back and dressed in a flurry. "Just when I thought I met a woman I could trust, another liar comes along and proves me wrong." He mounted his horse and refused to look at her.

"Go ahead. Run away. But someday Ryder Malone, you're going to have to face this—not just me, but the reasons you're so angry all the time."

He pushed the horse to a gallop, never looking back, the horse's hooves pounding on the hard path, blocking out whatever words she hurled at him. He'd done it again— he'd acted with his heart instead of his head.

When would he ever learn that women could never be trusted? Buried in the dark recesses of his memory was a thread of another thought that he wouldn't allow to weave its way forward, and it had to do with the first woman who had taught him this painful lesson.

Twelve

At dusk Essie raced to the stable and jumped off her horse, catching sight of Jenny, Shane and Josh, each holding the reins of their own horses.

Ryder's truck was nowhere in sight.

Good. Just the way she wanted it. If she was going to learn anything about this man, it would be easier if he wasn't around. She'd had the last couple of hours to think things through. She was tired of acting like a wimp. It was time to take matters in her own hands and resolve this thing with Ryder once and for all. If he wasn't going to get at the source of his anger, by golly, she was. She knew now how much she'd hurt him, both in high school and recently, but she also knew neither occasion initiated his problem. Maddy's dying words came back to her. *Ask him why he's angry with his mother.* If this was the source, she had to know, for Ryder's sake as much as her own.

Jenny ran up to her and pulled her into a tight embrace. "Sa—Essie! We were just about to go looking for you. Where have you been?"

Essie took in the worried faces and felt guilty for having caused such a stir. "I'm sorry. I just needed time alone. I didn't mean to worry anyone."

Shane stepped up and took her sorrel. "Glad you're okay, Essie." He led her horse away and gave Jenny a passing look.

Josh started to leave, but then Essie caught his sleeve. "Wait!" He looked back at her, startled. Shane stopped, too, and doubled back. "Can we talk for a while?" she asked, the quaver in her voice betraying her new confidence.

The brothers eyed each other, neither having a clue what subject she was about to broach. Seeming reticent, they turned and faced her.

"Sure," Josh said, while Shane simply stared.

"I'll wait inside," Jenny said, and started to go.

"Please stay." She took a deep breath and exhaled slowly, trying to dispel some of the tension she'd been feeling for the past couple of hours. She wanted Jenny here, for moral support, if nothing else. Besides, she would only have to repeat everything later.

"First, I may as well tell you." She glanced at Jenny, then back to the men. "My name isn't Essie. It's Savannah...Savannah Smith." She leaned on the last name and watched their faces turn from puzzlement, to suspicion, then finally shock. Josh was first to speak.

"*The* Savannah Smith? The one Ryder always talked about?" He looked her over from head to toe, as if seeing her for the first time.

Her gaze settled on Shane's impassive features. His arms were folded. He was waiting for the other shoe to drop. She directed her answer to him instead. "Yes. *The* Savannah Smith."

"Holy—" Josh took off his hat and beat it against a leg. "Does Ryder know?"

She held Shane's stare, but this time he answered first.

"Yes, little bro. He knows. Just this afternoon, right?" He glared at her, daring her to deny it.

She glanced at Jenny's pained expression, then back to Shane. "I had my reasons."

No one spoke for a while, as though digesting one thing before tackling whatever might come next. When she thought she'd waited long enough, she started to speak hesitantly, afraid of being stonewalled, but having to try.

"He's so angry—"

"Who wouldn't be," Shane said, interrupting her.

"No. I don't mean about me...about life in general. I want to help him, but I don't understand." Both men stared at their boots, their thumbs hooked in the backs of their jeans. "Please...can't you tell me something?"

A gravelly voice came from behind her. "He found her."

Startled, she turned to find Bucking Horse, his face in the shadows. "Please, Buck. Tell me more."

"It began with Max's time away. Ryder didn't understand."

"Who did?" Shane asked, his own anger showing through.

"Well, I did." Josh stood in front of his brother, fists on hips and leaned closer to Shane's face. "He's a doctor, for crying out loud. People depend on him...sometimes to save their lives. I didn't hear you complaining when he put us through college and he gave us all this." His arm swept wildly, gesturing to the house and the stables and the miles of land they called home.

Shane squared off in front of his brother. "It's easy for you to say. He was around more by the time you were born. But who was here the first time I fell off my horse?"

"I was," Buck said, stepping out of the shadows.

Shane looked at the old Indian, and Savannah noticed the anger on Shane's face slowly replaced with guilt. "Yes. You were."

"I did my best, Shane."

"I know." He kicked dirt, looking as though he would rather kick himself. When he looked up, there was pain in his eyes. "But why, Buck? Why did he stay away from me...from all of us so much?"

"It wasn't you or your brothers." Buck stood very still, his eyes focused on a spot between the men. "It was your mother he put moons between."

In her mind, Savannah heard Maddy's words again. Now she prayed Buck would provide the answer. No one asked the obvious next question, and for a moment she feared she might have to, but then Buck continued.

"She was like a wounded bird who couldn't fly. She would flap her wings...but always she would fall. Montana was not her land...never her home."

Besides the occasional nickering of horses around them, the stable stood silent, the only other sound that of secrets unfolding.

"Christina was a very beautiful, but spoiled, woman...first by her rich family, then Max." Buck lifted his face to the roof as if picturing her beyond. There was a glassy sheen over his eyes, and Savannah looked at Jenny, who gave a slight shrug, her eyes round.

"She would sit on the swing and cry...she thought no one could hear." Buck lowered his gaze and took in the brothers with a single glance. "I heard." The men stared back, their faces tense with anticipation. And for a moment Savannah wondered if Buck had ever said this many words at one time. She sensed he was on a mission and wouldn't stop till he finished. Without so much as a shuffle of boots, everyone watched and waited.

"Sometimes she would talk to me on that swing—" he motioned to the garden at the back of the house where an old glider still sat "—about the pain in her soul."

Shane folded his arms, drawing Savannah's attention. "You mean about the other women in Dad's life?" His tone reeked of bitterness; his jaw muscles flexed.

"Yes—" Buck paused and looked from one to the other, acting as though he'd just remembered they were listening to his words. Then he stunned both men. "And the other men in hers."

"No!" Josh closed the distance between himself and Buck. "You're lying."

Shane hung back and stared. On a whisper, holding the old man's weary gaze, he said, "Buck speaks the truth." The love and trust that traveled between the pair made Savannah look away. This was more than she wanted to learn. She hadn't meant to cause anyone pain when she'd started her quest, but just as she knew there was no going back, she knew there was more.

Josh was still in Buck's face. "Why would you tell us this...even if it's true?"

"Ryder must know."

Josh grabbed the old man's beaded vest with both fists. "Why? Why did any of this have to come out?"

Buck stood his ground, his posture and voice never changing. "Ryder blames your father for your mother's death. He saw his mother the innocent...your father the guilty."

Shane nudged his brother aside and stood toe-to-toe with Buck. "Go on."

"Max would never speak ill of your mother. He never spoke of her sins. He forgave her and tried again. More than many men would do." He fell silent awhile, and Savannah wondered if that was all. It was enough, by far. Many pieces were on the table now; it would be up to her to puzzle them out later, with Jenny, in the privacy of their room. But then Buck went on.

"Even when she cut herself, bleeding herself dry, Max did not tell."

"Why would he?" Josh asked, standing alone to the side, looking younger than his twenty-five years.

Shane ignored his brother's question and added to the pieces on the table. Never taking his eyes off Buck, he said softly, "He couldn't tell any of us about our mother's indiscretions without stealing the good memories we had of her. He'd rather we think badly of him than her."

Buck's smile was barely perceptible, but it was there. "Yes."

While the men's thoughts turned inward, Savannah walked quietly to Buck's side. Maybe enough had been told, but something Buck had said at the start of all this still hung in the air, unfinished. Shyly, she turned to him. "You said Ryder found her."

Buck closed his eyes for the longest time, and she thought he was ignoring her question. Slowly he raised his eyelids and met her gaze.

"Ryder loved his mother." He heaved a sigh and looked almost too tired to go on. "Every day he came home from school first. Often she would walk with him in the field...hand in hand...and they would talk. I do not know of what. But both seemed happy these times. Usually she met him at the door...I would see her kiss his cheek.

"That bad day...she wasn't at door...he went in." Buck closed his eyes again, and his body swayed. Shane reached out and held an arm, steadying him. Buck finished the rest with his eyes closed. "There was a howl—at first I think coyote—but coming from house. I run in. Young Ryder says words into telephone...then stares at bloody hands." He stopped swaying and opened his eyes, not seeing any of them. "I followed him down hall...past death room. He slid down wall...his hands dripping between his legs. I went in death room...she was already cold."

Jenny bent her head and slipped an arm around Savannah's waist. No one moved or spoke a word, waiting to see if there was more.

"To this day...I do not understand." Buck's face was gray, years of sun and wrinkles more apparent in his grief. "Why not Max find her? Or me? Why young Ryder who loved and trusted her so?" He shook his head slowly. "I can only think one way. At very end...her soul too sick...she could not see who would find her...who would suffer most...."

Maddy's and Buck's words linked in Savannah's head. *Find out why he's angry with his mother...Ryder loved and trusted her so.* Her heart ached, thinking of him finding her like that, as the last piece of the puzzle slipped into place. Savannah felt the tears on her face. If only he had told her in Detroit, when the pain had been new and not so deep-seated. How different would both of their lives have been all these years?

Buck's gaze passed to each of them, standing in front of him. He looked as though he was stunned that he wasn't alone. Without another word, he turned and walked slowly to his house. After taking care of the horses, Shane followed.

Josh still stared at his boots, not moving. When he spoke, it was more to himself than anyone. "Strange…how we all remember things a different way. I never blamed Dad for Mom's death. I always thought she was depressed and that one day she couldn't deal with it anymore." He looked up at Savannah and Jenny, who stood side by side with their arms locked around each other. His face looked older now. "I just thought she was a very sick lady…that it wasn't any of our faults. We all loved her, you know?" He didn't wait for an answer, but slowly made his way back to the main house.

Savannah watched him leave the stable and heard the squeak of the screen door shortly after. Jenny pulled her closer, and they stood there till dusk turned to blackness, then they went inside.

On Monday, the arrival of Ryder with Billy and all his worldly possessions did little to cheer the rainy morning. The boy moved through the house as if in a trance, carrying one box after another to his new room, his eyes cast down whenever he passed anyone in the hall. Savannah tried to help him, but Ryder let it be known they could manage just fine on their own. So she kept her distance, letting them settle in, biding her time.

At lunchtime, Ryder made a sandwich for Billy, ignoring Jenny and casting an occasional scowl in Savannah's direction, before taking a tray to his room.

By supper, Savannah was fuming. They needed to talk, and she couldn't wait much longer. Sure, he was angry with her, and justifiably. But in time he would come to understand her reasons for doing what she did, maybe he would even realize it was the only way. If she'd told him she was Savannah from the start, he may never have seen her as anyone other than an old friend.

And *simply friends* just didn't cut it. She wanted more. She always had. More to the point, now she knew he did, too, whether he was ready to admit it or not. If only she could get past his stubborn pride and make him see the true source of his pain. Still, how would she do that without maligning his mother? She'd seen the pain on Shane's and Josh's faces last night. She didn't want the same for Ryder.

She and Jenny had just finished the dishes when Savannah started pacing the width of the kitchen. "Jenny, Jenny, how am I going to do this? I can't just blurt out his mother wasn't the saint he thought she was. Besides, just because she was unfaithful, doesn't justify Max doing the same."

"No, but it equalizes things a bit. Maybe if Ryder knows, things won't seem as black-and-white as they used to. He certainly can't paint Max quite the villain he's made him out to be...once he knows."

"But if Max couldn't tell him about his mom for all these years, how can I, Jen?"

She rolled her eyes and folded her arms. "Yeah, you're right. It's probably better Ryder carry his anger to the grave...oh, and that you two never have a chance to be together...which of course means Billy will always have a dad with an attitude and little hope for a step-mom."

"You know, sometimes you really piss me off."

"Yeah, I know." She hiked one corner of her lip. "Especially when I'm right."

She stopped pacing and let out a loud sigh. "Okay, okay. I'll go talk to him. I don't know how much I'll tell him, but I'll try."

Jenny moved closer, resting her backside against the chopping block. "Boy, it sure is going to be dull making canapés back in Detroit."

"Then don't go back." Savannah rushed to her and placed both hands on her shoulders. "You can cook here as long as you want. I'm sure Max would agree."

"Nah." She broke the contact and started up the stairs. "You and Hannah can handle things. Max has been generous paying me, but he doesn't need three women on the payroll."

"Don't be so sure." Savannah followed her, not willing to give up. "Hannah's slowing down. Besides, she told me she prefers cleaning. And I'd rather spend seven days a week in the clinic than one in this kitchen. Come on, Jen. Stay."

She stopped on the landing before making the turn to their room. "I have several weddings booked...and there's still months left on the lease—"

"You could always sublet. If I have any luck with Ryder, you could have my room...or Shane's. He never uses it, anyway."

"Since when did you become such a pushy broad?" Jenny asked.

"Since the last twenty four hours—since I decided to go after what I want."

"Speaking of which, look." Jenny gazed out the small stairwell window and pointed to the swing in the backyard. The rain had finally stopped and Ryder sat on a towel, staring into space. "No time like the present."

She saw the hunch of his shoulders and her heart lurched. "All right. But don't think we're done with this conversation."

"We'll talk about it later tonight. Now go on."

Savannah followed the brick path leading to the swing in the yard, feeling as though she were Dorothy on her way to Emerald City. If she said the right words, all her dreams could come true. Yet she still had to deal with the volatile Wizard of Oz.

She tried to walk softly, but he heard her and cast a not-too-welcoming look over his shoulder.

"What do you want?" he snapped.

"To talk with you."

He stared straight ahead again. "There's nothing left to say."

She swiped at a puddle with a dish towel, then sat gingerly on the opposite end of the long swing, half expecting him to stalk away. When he didn't, she exhaled and began.

"I talked with your brothers and Buck last night…a-and I learned some things I think you should know."

"You what?" he shouted, springing from the swing as though shot from a cannon.

As difficult as it was, she met his angry glare and continued. "I wanted to know why you were so angry all the time."

He paced away, then stalked back. "What gives you the right to—"

She looked up at him and spoke softly. "I love you, Ryder. That's what gives me the right."

He kept breathing heavily, but this put a halt to his outburst. His fists dropped from his waist, and he slumped back onto the swing, sitting as far as he could from her, his face turned away.

"Please hear me out. If you don't like what I say, I'll never bring it up again. It's just that I—"

"Get on with it. Say what you have to say."

In a way it was easier speaking to the back of his head. She could imagine the anger, if not hatred, in his eyes this very moment. "Ever since I've known you, Ryder, you've blamed your father for everything—" she took a deep breath before adding the next part, a part she feared would make him bolt "—including the death of your mother." He didn't leave, but she saw the set of his shoulders and the muscles tightening on the side of his neck. Still she pushed on.

"Did you ever wonder if there was a reason Max spent so much time away?"

"I didn't have to wonder. Something kept him in Ann Arbor, and you didn't have to be a rocket scientist to figure it out. More lies and deception."

"But what about the time before that? Did you ever wonder if your mom—"

He spun on her, sending the swing careening at odd angles. "What in the hell are you suggesting?"

She braced herself and met his fury. "Ryder, I know you loved your mother, but when a marriage fails, it's rarely as one-sided as people think." She didn't want to tell him about his mother's infidelity; yet on the other hand, she didn't want a lifetime of anger ruining his chance for happiness, either, no matter how self-serving that might be.

He rested his elbows on his parted knees and stared at the ground between them. She wanted to rub his back, but she knew he'd shrug her hand away. She already knew the answer to the question she was about to ask, but she also knew it had to be said. It was now or never. She whispered the words softly, hoping he would hear the love in her voice.

"Ryder...why are you angry with your mother?"

He bounded from the swing, almost sending her to the ground, and headed for the house without acknowledging her question.

She dogged him all the way. "Buck told me you found her."

He lengthened his stride.

"I know how much it must have hurt you...she couldn't have known what she was—"

He stopped and spun on her, gripping her shoulders roughly. "You're the one who couldn't know what—" He dropped his hands and staggered backward, his face ravaged and raw. He turned and yanked open the screen door. She grabbed it before it closed and stayed right on his heels.

"Please don't shut me out. All I ask is that you think about it." He paused outside his door, his breathing labored. She tugged at his elbow, half turning him toward her. "If not for yourself, Ryder, then for Billy." She motioned with her head at the little boy she knew was on the other side of the closed door. For a second she saw something pass before Ryder's eyes—a flash of doubt, a seed of reason, but then Max raced down the hall from clinic and the moment was lost.

"Son, I could use your help," he said, breathless. "Got a big guy with a busted arm."

"I have to check on Billy." Ryder turned the doorknob, ignoring his father.

"Just for a while. He's had a few drinks and he needs restraining."

Savannah stepped in front of the door. "Please, Ryder, go help your father. I'll stay with Billy till you get back."

She could see the conflict in his weary eyes, but for once he didn't argue. Without a word he followed Max down the hall and out of sight.

Savannah hesitated only a moment, waiting for her pulse to slow before facing Billy. With a long sigh, she let herself in and looked around. A soft whimper came from somewhere, but Billy was no where in sight.

"Billy?" She tiptoed farther into his room, her gaze scanning the half-opened boxes and their contents strewn about the floor and bedspread. She heard a little sniffle coming from the far side of the bed. She walked around the end of it and found him sitting on the floor in the corner, his head on his knees, his arms hugging his legs. He looked up as she approached, tears streaking his freckled cheeks.

"I...I heard you and Ryder fighting." A hiccup made his little shoulders rise and fall.

"I'm sorry, Billy. We—"

He swiped his face dry and tried to sound tough. "It was about me, wasn't it?"

Savannah knelt on the floor in front of him. "Sweetheart...what would make you say a thing like that?"

He sat straighter, pushing his back against the wall, avoiding her eyes. "You know..."

She had thought he was grieving over Maddy, but now she knew it was something else. "No, Billy. I don't know. Tell me."

Still not looking at her, he said, "I used to hear people

laugh about me...they'd call me—'' another small sob passed his lips, and he looked embarrassed. ''They called me Bordello Billy.'' He braved a quick glance.

Savannah bracketed his head with her hands and spoke sternly. ''I don't ever want you to say that again, young man. Your name is Billy Malone—now and forever.''

His sad blue eyes filled with tears, the brave act disappearing. ''I—I don't know what it means, but I can tell it wasn't good—''

''Stop right there.'' She lowered her voice and looked him in the eye. ''Billy, it doesn't matter what people used to call you.'' She pointed to the area of his heart and tapped it lightly. ''It's who you are here that matters.'' Then she moved her finger to his forehead. ''And what you think about yourself there.'' She could see his mind working behind his big blue eyes, weighing her words, wanting to believe them. And while he struggled and she gave him time, she thought about the wisdom of her own words, about years of feeling like a worthless little fat girl, too often relying on others for her own self-esteem. The awareness seeped into her, and she felt stunned. Then Billy took her hand and she pulled herself back to his troubled little face.

''Honest? You weren't fighting about me...about not wanting me here?''

She pulled him to her at last, hugging him close and stroking his soft silky hair. ''Billy Malone, I never want you to think that again. We're proud to have you here. You know, Ryder didn't *have* to adopt you, little man. He *wanted* to.'' She gave him one last hearty squeeze, then set him apart from her.

''Now come on. Let's get this room whipped into shape and surprise him, okay?'' He nodded slowly. ''I'll find places for your clothes, and you find a home for all these posters and toys. Is that a deal?'' She pulled him to his feet in front of her. An image of his mother standing beside him flashed in her mind's eye and her heart ached for this little one's loss.

He looked up at her and finally showed her the gap in his front teeth. Shyly he stuck out his hand for a shake. "It's a deal."

Thirteen

Ryder held the unwilling patient in place and watched his father strap the broken arm to a side tray with speed and efficiency. The smell of alcohol emanating from the cowboy seemed enough to sedate a bear, and eventually the patient closed his eyes and gave up the struggle.

Ryder followed his father as he left the bedside and strode to the supply cabinet in the next room. He found a plastic-coated bag, tore open the top and dropped the contents in a round stainless steel basin. He glanced up and then returned to his task. "What is it, Ryder? You look like you have something on your mind."

He came right to the point. "I have a few questions...and I'd like some straight answers."

With his hand poised on the faucet, Max stopped and leaned against the counter. "All right. I'll do my best."

There seemed no point in being tactful. The question was bound to ruffle his feathers, anyway. "Did you ever cheat on Mom?"

Max took his time meeting his son's eyes. Quietly, he said one word. "Yes."

Ryder waited, wishing he would offer some excuse, anything, weak as it might be. But he didn't. He just stared at him, his expression contrite, begging for a forgiveness that Ryder didn't think he had in him.

"Was it with...was it...at the Purple Palace?" He couldn't bring himself to say Maddy. Though he'd never been with her himself, there was something perverse in thinking he'd almost married his father's lover.

Without hesitation and without breaking eye contact, Max answered. "No, Ryder. It wasn't."

Ryder felt his shoulders drop a notch.

"I won't deny I went over there from time to time. But only to have a few drinks, hear a few jokes. The girls made me laugh...forget for a moment about...well, about my troubles."

"May I ask who then?"

Max sighed and seemed to be weighing his choices. "There was a nurse in Ann Arbor when I taught there. It wasn't a fling, or whatever you'd call it. I cared about her a great deal."

"Then why didn't you leave Mom...stay with that—that nurse."

"Because I had a wife and sons who needed me more." There was no hesitation in his answer, but there was a hint in the depths of his eyes of how much that decision had cost him.

"Did Mom know?"

"No...at least I never told her. Whether she guessed or assumed, I'll never know. But, Ryder, our problems started long before that. Your mother never liked it here on the ranch. She missed the big city, the shopping, the parties. She wanted me to sell the ranch and move to Denver, near her family. In hindsight, maybe I should have—"

"Dad—" He swallowed hard, having to know, yet hating to ask. "Before Ann Arbor...was Mom unfaithful to you?"

For the first time his father looked away, the pain on his face answer enough. He turned on the water and filled the basin, his fingers working the bandaging he'd placed in it. When he turned back, there was a sadness in his eyes, one that cut straight through the wall Ryder had so carefully erected. Now, instead of seeing the self-centered person who had neglected his wife and children, he saw the heart of a mere man, imperfect as himself, wracked with guilt and regrets.

"I've never said an unkind word about your mother, Ryder. And I'd rather not start now. It's all so far in the past. Can't we leave it there?"

The fight had seeped from Ryder's soul, leaving him numb and exhausted. He'd held on to his hurt for so many years that it felt like an animate object, like a ragged old blanket he'd dragged around till nothing was left but shreds.

Something should be said here; what, exactly, he didn't know. Was it too late to begin again? Would he be able to reverse his old feelings for this man? Looking in his father's moist eyes, he felt a stir of something, maybe just empathy, but something that perhaps he could build on.

"Ryder...you have a son to raise now, and hopefully more in the future. What I wish for you—" he cleared his throat and looked away. "More than anything I wish you could enjoy your children...love them, truly love them... without bitterness in your heart."

There was a loud groan, followed by a string of curses from the patient in the next room. Max held Ryder's gaze and didn't move.

"Dad, I...I don't know what to say. I—"

Max wiped his hands on a towel, closed the distance between them and touched Ryder's shoulder. "Let's give it time, son. I'm not going anywhere. Are you?"

Ryder looked deeply into the eyes of the man he'd hated for so many years. Either this man was different now, or more likely, his middle son had finally grown up. "No, I'll be right here." There was another outburst from the next room, and Ryder nodded his head toward the patient. "You'd better go. Duty calls."

"You don't mind if we talk later?"

He wanted to pull the old man to him and reassure him, but he knew he'd make a fool of himself, and then the patient would suffer longer.

"No, Dad. I don't mind at all."

His father backed away slowly, taking the basin with him and looking as though he didn't want to leave. Then he turned and went to his howling patient.

Ryder didn't move a muscle, the effort seeming beyond him. Between his argument with Essie...or Savannah—he still couldn't get used to that—and now his father, he wondered how he would deal with Billy. The boy needed him. Getting him to leave his home at the Purple Palace had been more difficult than he had imagined. But consoling him now, seeing his tears, hearing his heartache, just seemed too much. He blew out hot air and threw his head back. "Maddy, Maddy. I hope you made the right decision leaving your son with this mixed-up cowboy."

Finally he pushed off the counter, left the clinic and wandered toward Billy's room. Before he got there, he heard loud squeals and shrieks of laughter, and a weight lifted from his shoulders. But when he got to the doorway, he couldn't believe his eyes. The boxes had been emptied and removed, posters hung from every wall, and the only things out of place were the two crazy people chasing each other with pillows stretched high over their heads. He leaned on the doorjamb and watched as Billy landed a solid blow on Savannah's hip. She let out a yelp and pursued him to the bathroom, where he was quick to shut and lock the door, giggling loudly from the other side.

"No fair. Come out and fight like a man," Savannah shouted through the door.

Ryder stared at her heaving back and listened to the giggles in the next room. Slowly the door opened and Billy came out, still breathing hard and with a gap-toothed smile from ear to ear. He spotted Ryder and ran to him.

"How do you like my room?"

Ryder wrapped an arm around the boy's shoulder and gazed down at him. "It looks terrific...son."

Billy blinked rapidly, his jaw dropping as he stared up the length of Ryder. "D-do you think...well...should I call you...Dad?"

The child's simple words were nearly his undoing. For a man who avoided emotion at every turn, today had been a marathon that he guessed was far from over. He cleared his throat. "Would you like to call me Dad?"

Billy tightened his hold on Ryder's leg and nodded. "Yes, sir...I mean...Dad." His smile widened, and Ryder had to look away. But when he did, he caught another pair of loving eyes, and he knew the last bricks had fallen from around his heart. How could he be angry with this woman? This woman who dragged him kicking and screaming into a world he had never embraced, a world he doubted he could be part of. There was so much he wanted to say to her, but for now he simply mouthed the words "Thank you" and watched the glow radiating from her face.

He squatted next to Billy. "Time to brush your teeth and get ready for bed."

The automatic frown and groan turned into a sweet smile. "Okay...Dad. But will you read to me, then?"

Ryder stood and turned him in the direction of the bathroom, giving him a gentle swat on the backside. "You bet."

He ran past Savannah, then doubled back, giving her a tight squeeze around the waist. "Thanks for helping me, Ess—I mean, Savannah."

She glanced at Ryder, looking somewhat surprised that he'd taken the time to tell the boy. Then she ruffled his hair. "My pleasure, Billy. See you in the morning." He stopped at the dresser and retrieved a folded pair of pajamas and then ran into the bathroom and shut the door.

Savannah put the pillows in place and started to leave. Ryder blocked the door. More than anything, he wanted to pull her into his arms, to tell her how grateful he was for not giving up on him, for loving him still. But Billy bounded out of the bathroom and hopped onto the bed. He was waiting for his story.

Ryder stepped aside and let Savannah pass, but not without a lingering look, one that he hoped she understood, that would tide her over till there was time to tell her all that was in his heart. She smiled as she left the room, and he listened to her footsteps fade away behind him.

"Well, don't you look like the cat that swallowed the canary!" Jenny teased, when Savannah sauntered into their room, her hands tucked behind her back hiding something.

With great flourish, she produced a bottle of wine and glasses from behind her. "I think it's time for a little celebration."

Jenny bounced on the middle of the bed and tucked her legs under her. "And to what do we owe the pleasure?"

Savannah poured a glass and handed it to Jenny, then poured a second, propped herself at the foot of the bed and offered a toast. "To life."

Jenny clinked her glass to Savannah's and said, "*L'chaem.* How's that for a nice Indian word?"

Savannah laughed. "Oh, you. I'm going to miss you, crazy person." She smiled, then sipped her wine.

"Who said I was going anywhere?" Jenny peered over her glass.

"I know you. You're going home Saturday, aren't you?"

"Yes, but you don't have to look so happy about it."

Savannah arched an eyebrow. "I also know you'll be back as soon as you tidy things up there." She watched her friend's expression and saw nothing that contradicted her statement.

"We'll see. Max said the job was mine, should I ever decide to come back." She held out her glass for a refill and cocked her head to one side. "Something's happened. What is it?"

"Oh, Jen. It's been such a miraculous day."

"Well, that's a relief. After the way Ryder acted on the

swing—'' She stopped and covered her hand. "Oops. Guess I was watching.''

Savannah laughed and shook her head. "The evening might have started out shaky, but it didn't end up that way.'' She wondered again what had happened to change Ryder's attitude. His whispered thank-you in Billy's doorway had to have meant more than appreciation for setting the room straight. Had he simply had time to calm down? Or had he and Max talked in the clinic? Either way, life was good.

"You were saying?'' Jenny eyed her over the rim of her glass.

"I think things are going to be okay with Ryder and me. More than okay. It might take some time for him to forgive me for my deception, but underneath it all, I know he loves me.'' Just saying the words aloud filled her to overflowing. It gave her a heady feeling, which, along with the wine, left her floating. "But something else wonderful happened, Jen.'' Setting her glass on the floor, she let her excitement flow through her hands as she told of Billy and their talk about self-esteem, the true reason for this little celebration.

"And here I was, in the middle of telling him it didn't matter what people said or thought about you, when I realized I'd been feeling that way all my life. Even after the braces and weight came off, I still felt like that unattractive little fat girl.'' Jenny leaned against the headboard and smiled. How many times had her friend tried to convince her otherwise over the years? Yet she had the grace now not to mention it. Instead, she relished the moment with her, true friend that she was.

"You should have seen Billy tonight, Jen. He was laughing and playing...and so adorable.'' She pictured the awe in his beautiful face when he looked up at Ryder and asked if he could call him Dad. And then she remembered the look in Ryder's eyes—the look of a proud and loving father. What *had* he and Max talked about earlier? Whatever it was, she prayed he would tell her eventually. For now it was enough to know something good had started between them. Of that, she was fairly certain.

"I'm happy for you, sweetie." Jenny finished her wine, not looking happy at all.

"Jen? What's wrong?"

"Just feeling a little blue about leaving this place. Who would have ever imagined I'd like a godforsaken place like Montana?"

Savannah swallowed a smug smile, remembering her prediction before this adventure ever began. "Are you sure it's Montana you're going to miss? Or could it have something to do with a certain cowboy? You know, you never told me much about that cattle drive you two went on." She slanted her a sly look.

"Shane?" She set her glass down and averted her eyes. "Nothing to tell. Besides…he lives with that spooky old Indian."

Savannah shook her head. When was her friend ever going to get past her prejudice? She seemed to think an entire race was responsible for abandoning her and her mother; instead, she should place the blame on the one person who did—her father.

"Every time I turn around, there he is, scaring the pants off me. I never hear him approaching. And don't you think it's strange that Shane lives out there with him instead of in here?"

"Not really. Shane was alone with Buck a lot growing up, especially those years when Ryder was in Detroit and Josh went to Denver to stay with his grandparents." She shrugged. "He probably felt more at home out there after so much time."

"Maybe." She reached for her glass and held it out. "Enough about Indians. Is there enough for another toast?" Savannah held the bottle to the light, then split what was left. "Here's to the best girlfriend I'll ever have. May all your dreams come true."

Savannah scooted closer and touched her glass. "Ditto, Jenny Moon."

* * *

Moonbeams filtered through the sheer curtains, sending shadows dancing against the ceiling and far wall. Savannah watched them and listened to the soft, steady breathing of the woman beside her. Not till today had she realized how dependent she'd been on Jenny and others to make her happy.

No longer was that true. A new inner peace filled her, and she lay there in the stillness enjoying it. For the first time in her life, she liked who she was. She would love it if Jenny returned. She would love it if Ryder married her and they lived happily ever after. But right now, at this very moment, she knew she could survive without either. And it empowered her like nothing else she had ever felt. She rolled on her side and punched the pillow, the smile slipping from her face as she drifted into a dreamless sleep.

Breakfast was on the fly all week as the men, accompanied by Billy, went about their chores, adding hours to the day with the long process of haying. For the next couple of months, they would be cutting hay and putting up round bales, weighing as much as fifteen hundred pounds, enough to feed the ranch's sixty brood mares and dozens of colts.

Billy was elated to be counted as one of the "men" and rode his paint pony proudly, usually too exhausted at day's end to dwell on the loss of his mother. Occasionally there were tears, and smiles were slow in coming, which everyone understood and respected. Hannah had given him a picture of a blond angel with big wings that she'd found, which now occupied the prime spot on the bulletin board near his bed.

After dinner each evening, an exhausted Billy would fall asleep before his dad ever finished a story, leaving Ryder and Savannah precious time to reminisce on the swing in the backyard. When they weren't recalling high school memories, they named constellations or simply listened to the sounds of the night and the creatures that roamed the wilderness beyond the ranch.

Eventually Ryder told her about his conversation with

his father and even talked about the early years with his mother. Savannah had long since apologized for her deceptive role as Essie, and had committed to total honesty from that point on; but sometimes she sensed he still hadn't completely forgiven her for her lies, which in part she understood, and which she suspected was his reason for not yet broaching the subject of marriage.

Friday night Savannah pulled her Michigan sweatshirt over her head and snuggled beneath Ryder's protective arm as he set the swing into motion. She sighed and gazed up. Even the full moon looked small in the vast Montana sky she had come to love. She thought if she sat here forever, she would never grow weary of this magical place and the feelings it evoked.

But their time tonight would be limited. Jenny was leaving in the morning, and Savannah would go upstairs soon and help her pack. They had agreed Shane would take her to the airport when the time came, sparing the women a prolonged farewell. Besides, it wasn't a time for sadness. Jenny would return in due time. Savannah was sure of it.

Ryder heaved a satisfied sigh, and she could tell something was on his mind.

"So Jenny was in on this little charade of yours from the start."

It was more a statement of fact, since he knew she was. Savannah sighed, thinking she'd been right, that he still hadn't worked past her role as Essie, though he sounded more teasing than angry tonight.

"Aren't you ever going to forgive me for all that?"

"Oh, I don't know." She could hear the smile in his voice as he pulled her closer. "Maybe I'll let you kiss up to me a bit longer."

She sat straighter and raised her chin. "You mean like this?" She pressed her lips to his and instantly forgot it was a game.

He kissed her long and deep, then nudged her back under his arm. "Something like that." He snickered. "We'll have to work on it." Somewhere a coyote howled at the moon, and they listened. Silhouetted in the distant glow was a lone deer or antelope. She couldn't tell which.

After a while, he said, "Tell me something."

"Hmm?" She wiggled closer and closed her eyes.

"Why did you hide your feelings for me in high school?"

"Are you kidding?" She batted at his chest playfully. "With all those skinny cheerleaders chasing after you?"

"Savannah, Savannah." He kissed the top of her hair. "Your figure had nothing to do with what attracted me."

"Attracted you?" She opened her eyes.

"Yeah, attracted me. I was crazy about you, and you should have known it wasn't just raging hormones, either. Hell, I even carved your initials into my headboard when I was home for summer vacation once."

She smiled into his chest, remembering her discovery. "I know. I saw it when I changed your sheets that first week."

"See? I have proof. But I guess I wasn't very good at expressing myself back then."

"I guess I wasn't ready to believe anyone could love me back then."

"And now?"

"Now I think you're one lucky cowboy."

His laugh was low and deep. She looked up into his dark eyes, slivers of moonbeams reflected there, and her heart beat faster. God knew she would always feel she was the lucky one, no matter how long it took for Ryder to forgive her. One day he would come around and let go of that last thread of anger...and she would be there, ready and waiting.

After breakfast the next morning, Savannah shooed Jenny away, insisting on cleaning the kitchen by herself. There were better things for her friend to do in what little time remained. She had just washed the counter when Ryder grabbed her from behind and spun her around. She let out a surprised squeal, then draped her arms over his shoulders and smiled up at him.

"I love you this morning," he said, kissing the tip of her nose.

"Good. Because I love you this morning, too." She pulled back from him, tilting her head. "Big on long-term commitments, aren't we?" He chuckled and locked his hands behind her waist, swinging her gently from side to side.

"Sounds to me like you're fishing for something more."

Her eyebrows shot up and she feigned shock. "Who, me?"

He smiled and kept rocking her. "I suppose I should ask you to marry me before Jenny leaves...so you can tell her the good news in person."

Savannah contained the excitement dancing through her veins, forcing herself to maintain the playful tone. She gazed at him sideways. "Hmm. A bit presumptuous, aren't you?"

He gave her a sly grin. "Am I?"

She lifted her chin and looked down her nose. "I guess you'll never know if you never ask."

Ryder heaved a loud sigh and made an exaggerated show of getting down on one knee and taking her hand in his. "Savannah Elizabeth Smith, will you marry me?"

Hannah burst into the kitchen, hands on hips and came to an abrupt stop. "Well, well!" She chortled and shook her head. "'Bout time ya got some sense in that thick skull of yers, Ryder Malone." She turned and started to leave, then threw a question over her shoulder. "Does this mean I'll never be able ta retire, or that Essie—I mean Savannah—is gonna kill us with her cookin'?"

They both laughed, Ryder coming to his feet. Savannah held tight to his hand and answered. "Neither, Hannah. You'll have to put up with my quick fixes for a while, but Jenny will be back...soon, I hope."

Hannah slapped her hands in a steepled position and looked to the heavens. "Praise the Lord." Then she looked back at them and said, "Well? What are ya waitin' fer? Don't let me interrupt nothin'." On that note she waddled around the corner.

When she was out of sight, Ryder pulled Savannah into his arms. "Well?"

"Well, what?" She grinned up at him, milking the moment for all it was worth.

"You didn't answer my question."

"Now, what do you think?"

"I think Billy could use a little brother or sister…or maybe a few of each."

"Whoa, cowboy. Slow down."

"Never." He thrust an arm under her knees and lifted her to him. "Where's Jenny?"

"At Buck's…spending her last hour with Shane." She kissed the side of his neck.

"Want to start now?"

"You mean in a bed this time? Do you think it will work there?"

"There…and anywhere else your beautiful heart desires."

She snuggled into his shoulder and let out a long, satisfied sigh. For the first time in her life she did feel beautiful. Gone was the insecure little girl and all that went with it. Here to stay was the woman she'd always wanted to be, the man she'd always loved and a whole new family that had come to feel like her own. Ryder paused at the bottom of the step and pressed his lips to her forehead.

Billy burst into the room and screeched to a halt, his rubber-soled sneakers squeaking on the wooden floor.

"Oops. Guess I came at a bad time." His cheeks went scarlet and he started to turn, bumping straight into Max, who was right behind him.

Max took one look at the situation, then bent to catch the boy's hand. "What say we go check on your pony?"

Billy looked up at Max, his cheeks fading to pink. "Okay…Grandpa."

Savannah looked from Ryder to Max then back, her heart melting, moisture stinging her eyes.

"Is it okay I call you Grandpa?" His gaze traveled up Max's long arm.

Max eyed Ryder as he answered the boy. "I'd be honored if you called me Grandpa, Billy." Ryder returned his father's smile as Max passed and headed for the stable, clutching Billy's hand.

Ryder held her close as he climbed the stairs to her room. Savannah nuzzled her head under his chin and thought about how far they had all come, her heart feeling as though it might burst with love and happiness.

She closed her eyes and thanked God for this magical spring and the wonders she'd witnessed. Lost love had been reborn—not just hers and Ryder's, but father's and son's.

And finally she thanked Him for Billy. The sweet little boy whose presence in her life had taught her so much about herself. The precious young son who with each passing day smiled more often, cocooned in the love of the Montana Malones.

* * * * *

This summer, the legend
continues in Jacobsville

Diana Palmer

A LONG, TALL TEXAN SUMMER

Three **BRAND-NEW** short stories

This summer, Silhouette brings readers a special
collection for Diana Palmer's LONG, TALL TEXANS
fans. Diana has rounded up three **BRAND-NEW**
stories of love Texas-style, all set in Jacobsville,
Texas. Featuring the men you've grown to love from
this wonderful town, this collection is a must-have
for all fans!

*They grow 'em tall in the saddle in Texas—and
they've got love and marriage on their minds!*

Don't miss this collection of original Long, Tall Texans
stories...available in June at your favorite retail outlet.

MILLION DOLLAR SWEEPSTAKES
OFFICIAL RULES
NO PURCHASE NECESSARY TO ENTER

1. To enter, follow the directions published. Method of entry may vary. For eligibility, entries must be received no later than March 31, 1998. No liability is assumed for printing errors, lost, late, non-delivered or misdirected entries.

   To determine winners, the sweepstakes numbers assigned to submitted entries will be compared against a list of randomly, preselected prize winning numbers. In the event all prizes are not claimed via the return of prize winning numbers, random drawings will be held from among all other entries received to award unclaimed prizes.

2. Prize winners will be determined no later than June 30, 1998. Selection of winning numbers and random drawings are under the supervision of D. L. Blair, Inc., an independent judging organization whose decisions are final. Limit: one prize to a family or organization. No substitution will be made for any prize, except as offered. Taxes and duties on all prizes are the sole responsibility of winners. Winners will be notified by mail. Odds of winning are determined by the number of eligible entries distributed and received.

3. Sweepstakes open to residents of the U.S. (except Puerto Rico), Canada and Europe who are 18 years of age or older, except employees and immediate family members of Torstar Corp., D. L. Blair, Inc., their affiliates, subsidiaries, and all other agencies, entities, and persons connected with the use, marketing or conduct of this sweepstakes. All applicable laws and regulations apply. Sweepstakes offer void wherever prohibited by law. Any litigation within the province of Quebec respecting the conduct and awarding of a prize in this sweepstakes must be submitted to the Régie des alcools, des courses et des jeux. In order to win a prize, residents of Canada will be required to correctly answer a time-limited arithmetical skill-testing question to be administered by mail.

4. Winners of major prizes (Grand through Fourth) will be obligated to sign and return an Affidavit of Eligibility and Release of Liability within 30 days of notification. In the event of non-compliance within this time period or if a prize is returned as undeliverable, D. L. Blair, Inc. may at its sole discretion, award that prize to an alternate winner. By acceptance of their prize, winners consent to use of their names, photographs or other likeness for purposes of advertising, trade and promotion on behalf of Torstar Corp., its affiliates and subsidiaries, without further compensation unless prohibited by law. Torstar Corp. and D. L. Blair, Inc., their affiliates and subsidiaries are not responsible for errors in printing of sweepstakes and prize winning numbers. In the event a duplication of a prize winning number occurs, a random drawing will be held from among all entries received with that prize winning number to award that prize.

5. This sweepstakes is presented by Torstar Corp., its subsidiaries and affiliates in conjunction with book, merchandise and/or product offerings. The number of prizes to be awarded and their value are as follows: Grand Prize — $1,000,000 (payable at $33,333.33 a year for 30 years); First Prize — $50,000; Second Prize — $10,000; Third Prize — $5,000; 3 Fourth Prizes — $1,000 each; 10 Fifth Prizes — $250 each; 1,000 Sixth Prizes — $10 each. Values of all prizes are in U.S. currency. Prizes in each level will be presented in different creative executions, including various currencies, vehicles, merchandise and travel. Any presentation of a prize level in a currency other than U.S. currency represents an approximate equivalent to the U.S. currency prize for that level, at that time. Prize winners will have the opportunity of selecting any prize offered for that level; however, the actual non U.S. currency equivalent prize if offered and selected, shall be awarded at the exchange rate existing at 3:00 P.M. New York time on March 31, 1998. A travel prize option, if offered and selected by winner, must be completed within 12 months of selection and is subject to: traveling companion(s) completing and returning of a Release of Liability prior to travel; and hotel and flight accommodations availability. For a current list of all prize options offered within prize levels, send a self-addressed, stamped envelope (WA residents need not affix postage) to: MILLION DOLLAR SWEEPSTAKES Prize Options, P.O. Box 4456, Blair, NE 68009-4456, USA.

6. For a list of prize winners (available after July 31, 1998) send a separate, stamped, self-addressed envelope to: MILLION DOLLAR SWEEPSTAKES Winners, P.O. Box 4459, Blair, NE 68009-4459, USA.

SWP-FEB97

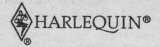

And the Winner Is... You!

...when you pick up these great titles
from our new promotion at your
favorite retail outlet this June!

Diana Palmer
The Case of the Mesmerizing Boss

Betty Neels
The Convenient Wife

Annette Broadrick
Irresistible

Emma Darcy
A Wedding to Remember

Rachel Lee
Lost Warriors

Marie Ferrarella
Father Goose

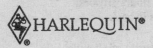

Look us up on-line at: http://www.romance.net   ATWI397-R

National Bestselling Author

JoANN ROSS

does it again with

NO REGRETS

Molly chose God, Lena searched for love and Tessa
wanted fame. Three sisters, torn apart by tragedy,
chose different paths…until fate and one man
reunited them. But when tragedy strikes again,
can the surviving sisters choose happiness…with
no regrets?

Available July 1997 at your favorite retail outlet.

MIRA The brightest star in women's fiction

MJRNR

Look us up on-line at: http://www.romance.net

New York Times Bestselling Authors

JENNIFER BLAKE
JANET DAILEY
ELIZABETH GAGE

Three *New York Times* bestselling authors bring you three very sensuous, contemporary love stories—all centered around one magical night!

It is a warm, spring night and masquerading as legendary lovers, the elite of New Orleans society have come to celebrate the twenty-fifth anniversary of the Duchaise masquerade ball. But amidst the beauty, music and revelry, some of the world's most legendary lovers are in trouble....

Come midnight at this year's Duchaise ball, passion and scandal will be...

Unmasked

Revealed at your favorite retail outlet in July 1997.

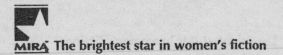